HAMPSHIRE
FOLK TALES
FOR CHILDREN

HAMPSHIRE FOLK TALES FOR CHILDREN

MICHAEL O'LEARY

ILLUSTRATED BY SU EATON

The History Press

For Eddie and Alice

First published 2016

The History Press
The Mill, Brimscombe Port
Stroud, Gloucestershire, GL5 2QG
www.thehistorypress.co.uk

British Library Cataloguing in Publication Data.
A catalogue record for this book is available from the British Library.

ISBN 978 0 7509 6484 5

Typesetting and origination by The History Press
Printed in Great Britain

CONTENTS

ABOUT THE AUTHOR AND ILLUSTRATOR

MIKE has been a professional storyteller for over twenty years, but has been telling stories since he was a toddler, when he claimed that the puddle on the floor was created by the wind. He collects stories from under stones, behind walls and wherever he happens to fall over them.

SU is a New Forest-based artist, hurdy-gurdy player and performer with Hand to Mouth Theatre. She has endeavoured to weave a creative way through life, illustrating her experiences – and sometimes those of other people – along the way.

1

THE APPLE TREE MAN

As this is a book of folk tales, I would like to start by explaining to you what a folk tale is. The trouble is, I'm not really sure.

I think the best way to put it is to imagine someone telling a story to their children, and then those children grow up and tell the story to their children. Then they grow up, and … on and on through the generations. Some bits of the story might remain the same, whilst others change like Chinese whispers.

(Chinese whispers. Do you know the game? You sit in a circle and someone whispers a sentence to the person sitting next to them. It goes round the circle, and when it gets back to the beginning again, everyone hears how the sentence has changed.)

The trouble is, I've just told you that a folk tale is something old, or at least a story from some time ago, but I'm about to tell you a story about something that happened to me. But then, I suppose, I am old – and it did happen a long time ago; back in the 1970s.

Back then I had black hair; it's white now, and given that I'm 63 years old you may think that's not surprising. But the thing is it turned white when I was still a young man in my twenties, and it did it overnight. In the evening it was black, and in the morning it was white. I'll tell you what happened.

I worked as a greenkeeper – that is, I worked on a golf course, cutting the grass, putting in drains – all sorts of jobs. When I started there we were building the golf course. I never really understood golf, but I liked working outside in the open air. In some ways, though, it struck me as a shame that land that used to be a farm was being turned into a golf course, but then I suppose I was part of that process too.

Now – next to the golf course there lived an old man called Jim Privet; he was 96 years old, and he'd worked on that land, when it was a farm, for all of his life. I loved to listen to the stories he used to tell about how life had changed in the Hampshire countryside over all those years.

Jim lived in a red-brick Hampshire cottage with roses growing around the front door, and the cottage was next to Sandy Lane. Sandy Lane was a sunken lane. This means that people had walked along it, and hauled their carts along it, for years, for generations, and over time it had sunk below the ground. Trees and bushes and brambles grew along the sides, and sometimes they met at the top, making the lane feel like a tunnel. That's why people sometimes call them 'holloways', which is short for 'hollow ways'.

Jim never could get used to some of the new farming methods. Whilst he was working on that farm, farmers started using more and more herbicides (weedkillers), and more and more insecticides (insect killers), and Jim used to have to spray them on to the crops. When the nozzles – the little holes that the spray came out of – got blocked up, Jim would put the end of the sprayer into his mouth and blow through it in order to clear them. This was a very bad idea. The herbicide and insecticide got into Jim's lip and started to rot it away. Jim had to go to the hospital in Winchester and have his lip cut off. They then pulled the skin up over his gums, because he didn't have any bottom teeth left. This gave Jim's face a pointy, distorted look. Jim used to wear an old-fashioned hat, he had big, bushy eyebrows, and he used to smoke a pipe, containing very strong tobacco. You could smell when Jim was coming down the lane because you could smell the tobacco smoke.

My mate, who everyone calls Digger, lives at the end of Sandy Lane, and he says that sometimes, when he's walking the dog in the evening, he smells the tobacco smoke. He turns round, expecting to see old Jim, then thinks, 'Jim's been dead for more than thirty years.' Digger says that Jim's ghost still walks Sandy Lane, still smoking that pipe. I think Digger is pulling my leg, because he always did like teasing people and making up stories, but you can still sense Jim's presence in the lane.

Anyway, one evening back in the 1970s, Jim and I went for a pint of beer or two at a pub called the Wheatsheath. It was late when we wandered back down Sandy Lane. At that time I lived in a caravan with my wife Cathy. In order to get back to the caravan I had to climb over a gate, and walk through an orchard – lots of old apple trees. Behind the orchard there was a pond called Basil Gamblin's pond, because it was owned by a farmer called Basil Gamblin. It was a bit of a dreary old place, all surrounded by elder bushes.

Jim and I stopped by the gate, which had a stone post at one end, and a stone post at the other end. I probably shouldn't say this, but I piddled on one stone post, and Jim piddled on the other stone post. Drinking beer always makes you piddle a lot.

Well, after that we were leaning on the gate and talking about this, that and the other, when Jim said to me, 'Have you ever heard tell about wassailing the orchard?'

No – I hadn't.

'Years ago,' Jim continued, 'on Twelfth Night everyone used to go up to the orchard at midnight. Twelfth Night is twelve nights after Christmas, the old New Year. We'd make a lot of noise, we'd fire shotguns into the air, we'd bang pots and kettles together, and we'd ring bells. Then we'd get some cider, the drink made out of apples, and we'd pour it around the roots of the big tree in the middle of the orchard, that's the tree that everyone used to call "The Apple Tree Man".'

'What was all that for?' I asked.

'It was to drive the evil spirits out of the orchard, to bring good luck, and make sure that when next autumn came there'd be good, juicy apples growing on the trees.'

I found all this really interesting, because I like to hear the old stories. But then Jim said a strange thing.

'Whatever you do, nipper,' – Jim called everyone that was younger than him 'nipper', and given that he was 96 years old, that was everyone except Mr Baker, who was 102 and lived down in Wickham – 'Whatever you do, nipper – don't take the shortcut through the orchard tonight. It's Twelfth Night, and it's midnight. No one has wassailed the orchard for years and years, so if you go through there tonight, you'll upset the Apple Tree Man.'

Now, I thought that Jim was joking. He was worse than Digger for pulling people's legs.

'Yeah, all right Jim,' I said, 'but you know that's my shortcut home.'

'I'm not joking, nipper,' he said, 'no one has wassailed the orchard since the 1920s. A lot of the men never came back from the First War, and the custom died out. So if you go through there tonight, you'll upset the Apple Tree Man.'

Well, I still thought that Jim was joking, so I repeated, 'Yeah all right Jim, but you know that's my shortcut home.'

Jim suddenly got really angry: 'You nippers!' he shouted. 'You think you know it all – go on then, find out for yourself' – and he went stamping off down Sandy Lane in a very bad mood.

'Oh dear,' I thought. 'I didn't want to upset him. If I knew he was going to react like that, I would have taken the long way home. Oh well, he's gone now, so I might as well take the shortcut.'

So I climbed over the gate and started to walk through the orchard.

It was a neglected orchard, which means that no one really looked after it any more. Usually people have 'thinned the trees out', which means that they've removed some branches in order to make room for other branches to grow, but these trees hadn't been worked on for years, and they were all twisty and tangled. There was a bit of a breeze blowing, not a strong wind, just a breath, but the branches were creaking and groaning.

Then I got up to the big tree in the middle of the orchard – that's the one they call the Apple Tree Man. Apple trees have got rough, knobbly trunks, and there are always knot holes that look like ancient faces.

'Oooh,' I thought, 'this is spooky – come on, don't be silly, just keep walking.'

So I did.

Then I had that feeling that we've all felt one time or another. The feeling that there was someone behind me, watching me. This was when I felt something grasp my shoulder – and when I looked at my shoulder I saw something that looked like a hand; and yet … not a hand; it was all knobbly and gnarled like the branch of a tree.

SLOWLY – slowly – I looked round. I found myself looking straight into the face of the Apple Tree Man. I don't know what you would do, but I'll tell you what I did. I SCREAMED.

I turned, and I ran and I ran and I ran, with my hair standing on end. When I got to Basil Gamblin's pond, round the back of the orchard, what did I see? Lots of black cats flying around on broomsticks. So I SCREAMED again, ran across the fields, and back to the caravan.

'Whatever's the matter with you?' said Cathy. I couldn't answer; I just sat there for an hour, gibbering. It took another hour for my hair to stop standing on end, but when it

did – it had turned white. So if you ever meet me you'll see that my hair is white, and that will prove to you that this story is not a fib. You see, unlike Digger or Jim Privet, when I tell stories, they are always true.

2

THE
BURLEY
DRAGON

In the New Forest (which isn't new at all) there is a village called Burley. Burley is a popular tourist spot, and is full of shops selling all sorts of 'witchy' stuff: witches' hats, broomsticks, mini cauldrons, cuddly witch toys, crystals, and the like. This is all because a lady called Sybil Leek lived there in the 1950s; she used to be on the radio (we called it the wireless in those days) talking about witchy things, and she used to write books about spells and suchlike. She walked around the village wearing a long black cloak and with a jackdaw on her shoulder. As you can imagine, this attracted a lot of interest. Some of the villagers didn't like it, but others thought they'd be able to make a few quid out of this, selling stuff to the tourists. Sybil Leek got fed up with the place and went to America, but now Burley is full of witchy shops, and I think that it's all good fun – though it would be a great shame to just go to the Burley shops, and not into the forest itself.

Maybe, though, Burley should really be associated with dragons rather than witches – because there is a dragon story there that is much, much older than all that witchy stuff.

This story is set in a 'Once upon a time' sort of a time – and in that time a dragon lived on top of Burley Beacon. Burley Beacon is a ridge of land overlooking the Avon Valley – rich fields and farmland spread along the banks of the Hampshire Avon, a river that flows along the western edge of the New Forest.

The dragon would hunt for his food in the forest – he'd catch hedgehogs, rabbits, badgers, owls and foxes – just a blast of fiery dragon breath and he'd bring them down, ready cooked. Hedgehogs were the nicest, providing he opened them up and sucked the meat out from between the spines – but a dragon would have to eat ten of them to have as much as a snack. I mustn't exaggerate the size of a dragon – modern authors and film-makers tend to portray them as being as big as mountains, but I've seen dragon fossils at Marrowbones Hill, which is on the eastern side of the forest near Foulford Bottom, and they don't get much bigger than a large bull. Mind you, if you have a fire-breathing dragon, as big as a bull, charging at you out of the woods, or swooping down at you from the sky, then that really must be terrifying enough; they don't have to be the size of a jumbo jet.

For a dragon, a badger made a much better-sized meal than a hedgehog, but badgers don't taste very nice – the meat is strong and rank, and the smell is rancid.

What the dragon liked best was wild boar. Wild boars are huge, so they make a most satisfying meal – and they taste wonderful. Hog roast with crackling, and if you've never tasted wild boar flame-grilled with dragon fire then I'm afraid you've missed a treat.

There was a problem with wild boars, though – they were liable to fight back. Not only were they huge, sometimes even bigger than a dragon, they had razor-sharp tusks, massive, powerful heads and jaws, and they were covered in sharp bristles.

The Burley Dragon had experienced a lot of trouble from wild boars. In spite of his advantages – being able to fly and breathe fire – they had sometimes thundered out of the trees so fiercely and fast that they'd caught him a proper thump before he'd had time to react – and those tusks were even capable of piercing dragon scales. One particular boar, a huge monster of a beast, had started to take grim pleasure in tormenting the dragon, and had once caught him unawares by charging in from behind and butting him with such force that the dragon wished he was able to blast fire out of his bottom. It almost felt that he had – he was certainly unable to sit down for a month.

The dragon really wasn't very brave – well, creatures that have scales and that can fly and breathe fire generally don't need to be brave – and it started to think that hunting wild boars was much too risky, but there was nothing else that really made a decent meal.

One day, as it sat on Burley Beacon, gazing out over the Avon Valley, it started to wonder about those green fields full of sheep and cattle. You see, it didn't normally leave the New Forest. All around the edge of the forest there is an invisible line called 'The Perambulation' – and New Forest dragons never crossed it. They didn't know why, they just knew that they shouldn't.

The dragon was suffering from indigestion after eating a particularly rancid, partially flame-grilled badger. As he gazed wistfully at the sheep and cattle in the fields, wondering what they tasted like, there was a whole lot of crashing and grunting, and that enormous wild boar came charging out of the forest, head down, tusks pointing forward, intent on giving the dragon's bottom a particularly nasty wallop.

'That's it,' thought the dragon, 'I've had enough – stupid forest, stupid wild boar, stupid, rancid badgers. I'm off,' and he spread his wings and soared up and away from Burley Beacon. He crossed the perambulation of the New Forest and nothing happened, nothing seemed to change.

'This is great,' he thought, so he swooped down over a field and ate a sheep. It was delicious. So he ate two more.

Then he lay down on his back, burped, flapped his wings lazily, and had a snooze.

He woke up to the sound of shouting, so he raised his head and saw lots of peasants, standing behind a hedge, swearing at him and waving pitchforks, prongs and assorted agricultural implements in a very angry manner. He looked at them and roared (and it was only a little roar), and they all turned tail and ran away.

'This is easy,' thought the dragon, and flew back to Burley Beacon – circling it a few times to make sure that the wild boar was gone.

Well, after that he continually raided the farm, which was called Lower Bisterne Farm.

It just seemed so easy. He discovered that beef was delicious too, in a different way to mutton – but the pork – oh that was the best. The pigs would grunt and try to fight back a bit, but they were nothing compared to a wild boar, and they were so soft and tender – and the crackling: it was simply divine.

As for the humans, well they always ran away and hid. He caught and ate one once, but it was disgusting and tasted of wee-wee.

Then the dragon started to experiment. If you glided over the banks of the Avon and skimmed off a whole load of water mint, and put it on to a sheep after giving it a blast of fiery breath, it greatly enhanced the taste, as did horseradish with the cows. Best of all, though, was to shake the apples off the trees in the orchard, and eat them with the pigs. That was just so delicious it made the dragon's claws curl.

The dragon started to attack all the farms down the Avon Valley, and there was uproar from the village of Blissford to the village of Winkton. It continued to pick on Lower

Bisterne Farm, though, and the people there were at their wits' end. They started to put out buckets of milk, hoping that this would satisfy the dragon so that he would leave them alone. He knew what they were doing, so sometimes he would drink the milk (which was delicious) and then fly back to Burley Beacon, just to encourage them to put out more milk. But just when they started to think he was going to leave them be, he'd be back again and eat more sheep, or cows, or pigs – and once he ate a goat, which was all right, and a donkey, which was disgusting.

Well, Lower Bisterne Farm was broken – the livestock was all gone, there weren't even any cows to give the milk to try to satisfy the dragon, and the people didn't dare to go out to the fields to work. The dragon was now raiding the other farms, and the people knew that unless they took action, they would all starve.

So they collected up as much money as they could, and sent word all the way up to Berkeley in Gloucestershire. In Berkeley there dwelt a dragon fighter, a professional, a lone dragon assassin, a slayer of monsters. It was a tough job, and a lonely one, but someone had to do it – and his name was Sir Maurice de Berkeley.

Sir Maurice and his two great wolfhounds travelled all the way down to Hampshire, and the knight rented himself out a nice little cottage at Moyle's Court (he'd charge it to expenses). Next he hired a little orphan boy called Perkin Purkis to be his assistant, and Perkin Purkis was glad of the work.

'First thing we have to do, Master Perkin,' said Sir Maurice, 'is make a goodly batch of bird lime.'

Now some people think that 'bird lime' means bird poo, but thankfully for Sir Maurice, it doesn't. It is a bit smelly though, and birds hate it. This is because it is sticky, gooey stuff that people used to spread on the branches of trees in order to catch birds – they would alight on the branch and get stuck. Sir Maurice, however, had no intention of catching birds; he was after something much bigger.

It takes a while to prepare bird lime. Firstly Perkin and Sir Maurice had to gather lots of holly bark, and there's plenty of that in the New Forest; then they had to boil it in a big pot for a whole day. It made the cottage stink something chronic, and the landlady thought, 'Oh Lor, whatever are they doing?' but everyone wanted to be rid of the dragon, so no one asked any questions. After this the dragon fighter and his assistant stored the pot of stinky stuff in the larder for two weeks, during which time it got stinkier and stinkier. After this they mixed in a lot of pounded-up acorns and conkers, and boiled it all up again. Now it stank so much that the dragon, snoozing up on Burley Beacon, was woken by the smell.

Then Sir Maurice got a load of bottles of beer from the nearby Ringwood Brewery and drank it all, after which he and Perkin set about smashing all the bottles.

'Oh Lor, oh Lor,' moaned the landlady, hearing the smashing sound of bottles being hurled around inside her cottage, accompanied by the barking and howling of the dogs.

'Time for me to don my armour, boy,' roared Sir Maurice, 'but first, after drinking all that beer I must have a pee.'

So after Sir Maurice had had a piddle in the middle of the griddle, Perkin helped him on with his armour. Perkin then took a brush and a shovel and covered Sir Maurice from head to foot with bird lime. After this he shovelled up all the broken glass and chucked it all over the noble knight's armour, where it stuck fast.

They then tethered a pig to a post, and Sir Maurice strode forth to do battle, his great dogs running ahead of him, whilst little Perkin Purkis watched from behind a hedge.

Truth be told the dragon was attracted as much by the smell of the bird lime as by the thought of a hog roast, and he came flapping down from Burley Beacon as much out of curiosity as hunger.

Instantly Sir Maurice's brave dogs threw themselves at the dragon. They were tough and fast, but the dragon tore them to pieces, and flung them contemptuously to one side – something that made little Perkin cry, because he'd grown to love those dogs.

Then the dragon roared, blew out a great ball of fire, and leaped on Sir Maurice. The battle lasted all day – every time the dragon coiled around Sir Maurice, the broken glass tore at its scales, and the bird lime pulled and ripped at its skin. Sir Maurice jabbed and sliced with his sword, until the dragon was as filled with holes as a pincushion.

As the evening drew in the two of them lay exhausted, and as they did so, Sir Maurice's helmet fell off and rolled down the slope. The dragon lifted its head ready to strike the final blow, whilst also roasting Sir Maurice in his own armour. It was then that little Perkin Purkis ran forward brandishing a tree-felling axe, and chopped off the dragon's head.

And that was the end of the dragon. Sadly, Sir Maurice died shortly after. He had suffered greatly in the battle, both from his wounds and from the poisonous effects of dragon blood. He was buried with his dogs, somewhere with the forest behind and the waters of the Hampshire Avon in front. No one felt sadder than little Perkin Purkis, though to him the death of the dogs was the saddest bit.

I don't know where the grave is, but I know that at Bisterne Manor House there is a stone carving of a dragon between fiery beacons, and a coat of arms with a dragon crest: the Berkeley Arms. Looking out over the entrance to the house there are two great stone dogs, surely statues of Sir Maurice's hounds. There is also a patch of ground in Dragon Field, Lower Bisterne Farm, where the grass will never grow. This is, of course, because it has been poisoned by dragon blood.

3

THE
WHERWELL
COCKATRICE

Wherwell is a peaceful village, spread along the banks of the River Test. To sit there and listen to the bubbling of the river and the bells of Wherwell Priory ringing across the water meadows would give anyone a feeling of peace and tranquillity.

You wouldn't feel very tranquil, though, if the Wherwell cockatrice was around. The cockatrice was a monster, and it ate people. If you were to meet it, it would be quite happy to eat you. All up.

It was a sort of dragon – a chicken dragon – because it had the body of a dragon and the head of a chicken, well, not a little fluffy chick, but a cockerel. It was a very strange beast, but this *is* Hampshire.

The story starts with a hen, and she was so proud of herself after laying her first egg. She clucked and chuckled and paraded around the farmyard, as if to say 'Look at me – look at me' to the other hens, who turned their beaks up into the air, to show that they'd seen it all before.

It was whilst she was parading around that a toad came creeping towards the hen's egg.

Toads don't keep their eggs, they lay them in long strings by the riverbank and leave them, but this toad wanted an egg. To her, a hen's egg was a giant egg, and she wanted a giant egg. So she pushed the egg out of the chicken pen, rolled it across the farmyard, down some steps, and into a cellar underneath Wherwell Priory. The toad then squatted over the egg – and the egg incubated, warmly and damply. When the egg tore open (it was too damp to crack) out came a cockatrice. When a hen's egg is incubated by a toad, the result is always a cockatrice. At least, that's what the stories say!

Underneath the priory, the cockatrice grew and grew, and the nuns at their devotions little knew that there was a monster growing beneath them.

The mother toad brought the cockatrice lovely tasty snacks: woodlice, slugs, worms, spiders, snails and centipedes. The cockatrice continued to grow until it was bigger than the toad, and then it ate her too, which really wasn't very nice. It then crawled out of the cellar, up the steps, and out into the sunshine. Ouch – it hated the sunshine – it stung.

So the cockatrice, now as big as a dog, found a nice hollow place by the river. It stopped crawling and started to run – though it never went far from its hollow – which it dug deeper and deeper – and which filled with water, but the cockatrice liked that.

It ate ducks and swans, and grew quite good at flicking fish out of the river. When it had grown to the size of a horse, it chased a nun across a field and ate her too.

That was too much – the Prioress of the Priory and the Bishop of Winchester, who was very important, strode across to the cockatrice, and commanded it to stop.

It ate them.

Well, eating people was bad enough – but eating the cattle, sheep, goats and pigs on the farms was worse, because that was people's livelihoods. It was as bad as the Burley Dragon – poor Hampshire, to be beset by such beasts.

So the people called on their local lord, the noble Sir Eginard the Unwieldy of Nether Wallop.

'Come thou forth, Sir Eginard,' cried the people. 'You're happy to take our tithes and taxes, now you've got to give us a bit of protection.'

So, Sir Eginard donned his armour, saddled up his noble steed, and rode to the field, next to the River Test in Wherwell, wherein dwelt the cockatrice.

He reined in his horse at the opposite side of the field from the river, and bellowed, 'Cockatrice, show thyself!' The cockatrice lifted its head and glared at Sir Eginard.

'Prepare to meet thy doom!' shouted Sir Eginard, levelling his lance.

'Cockadoodleburp,' said the cockatrice.

'Hast thou nothing better to say to a knight, he who hast come to rid the earth of thy pestilential presence?' roared Sir Eginard.

The cockatrice lifted its bottom out of the hole, screwed up its eyes, and let out a long, smelly, wet one.

'Have at thee, foul fowl from hell!' shouted the outraged Sir Eginard, and galloped straight at the cockatrice.

The cockatrice turned round, opened its beak, and ate Sir Eginard up – armour, horse and all.

'Doodle-doo,' it squawked, and spat the armour out. It then ran along the riverbank and ate two sheep in order to take the taste away.

Well, the people were at their wits' end. They sent messages out far and wide – there was a reward for slaying the cockatrice. Sir Egbound the Uncomfortable came all the way from Egdon Heath in Dorset, and got eaten; Sir Egregious the Untruthful came down from London, and got eaten; and Sir Egnog the Unsteady came riding in from Old Basing, and got eaten. After that the knights stopped coming; they left Wherwell to the cockatrice.

But then, a travelling tinker man brought the news to a faraway village in Sussex, called Dragons Green. In Sussex they have dragons that they call 'knuckers' – dragons that live in deep, deep ponds called Knucker Holes – and a young man from Dragons Green, called Egbyrt Green, was making a bit of a living from fighting them (that is, on top of his regular job as a baker). He had never had dealings with a cockatrice though, so he told the people of Dragons Green that they'd have to bake their own bread for a few months, gathered up his dragon-fighting equipment, wrapped it all in a spotty hankie, tied the hankie to a stick, slung the stick over his shoulder, and set off for Hampshire.

'I've come to slay thy cockatrice,' he announced to the people of Wherwell, as he entered the White Lion Inn.

'Where do you come from?' asked the suspicious locals.

Egbyrt puffed out his chest. 'I'm from Sussex,' he announced proudly.

'Bloody foreigner,' said a grumpy-looking man, leaning on the bar, 'the like of thee'll never kill our cockatrice. It ate Sir Eginard himself, and 'tis twice as big as them silly little knuckers down in Sussex, you.' (Hampshire people always used to put the word 'you' at the end of a sentence. They don't now; I don't know why they stopped – probably through watching too much telly.)

Egbyrt Green started to get the impression that the people of Wherwell were almost proud of their cockatrice, even though it was eating them out of hearth and home.

'Well, I shall slay your cockatrice,' he said, 'because I've got brains as well as brawn,' and the assembled Hampshire people weren't bright enough to work out that he'd insulted them. A well-known poem used to be:

I'm Hampshire, born and bred,
Strong in the arm, and thick in the head.

Well, Egbyrt Green had a few pints of Wherwell cider, and then he went down to the cockatrice's field. He undid the spotty hankie, and took out a big, round mirror. He polished it with his hankie, attached a chain to it, and then lowered it down the hole in which dwelt the cockatrice. The smooth face of the mirror slid against the cockatrice's face, then bumped its back. Its eyes opened. 'What's this? What's this?'

Using his other arm, Egbyrt lowered a lantern on a chain. In the light of the lantern the cockatrice caught sight of its own reflection.

'Another cockatrice,' it thought. 'I'm the only cockatrice in Wherwell – who is this upstart?'

And then it set about the mirror. All day it fought its own reflection – well, truth be told, it was a Hampshire cockatrice and not any brighter than the people, so it fought itself all day and all night before it was completely exhausted, at which point Egbyrt climbed into the hole, and, with a Sussex woodsman's axe, chopped off the cockatrice's head.

And do you know what? I feel sorry for the cockatrice. I know it went around eating people and stuff, but we eat chickens, and we should really be able to think about these things a bit more than a cockatrice can.

Anyway, Egbyrt claimed the reward. The reward turned out to be four acres of land in nearby Harewood Forest – and land is worth more than mere money any day. To this day the land is known as Green's Acres.

Egbyrt Green went back to Dragons Green, sold his bakery to a man called Jim Pulk, and went back to Hampshire to work his land. His ancestors lived there for centuries, but then the house prices got very expensive, so the Wherwell Greens sold their houses and moved into the nearby town of Andover. I believe that the Green family live there still.

As for the cockatrice, it was stuffed and its body put on display in the White Lion. It got a bit smelly, and the feathers all fell out, so in the end they had to burn it on a bonfire. They did make a cockatrice weathervane, though, and it was put on to the church tower. It scared people, so it got taken down, and now it's in Andover Museum. If you don't believe me, go and have a look.

4

BEVOIS
OF
SOUTHAMPTON

This story starts in Scotland, in a gloomy castle, on a gloomy headland, overlooking the dark North Sea. This was the gloomy place where a gloomy girl called Murdina grew up. I'm not surprised she was gloomy, because being brought up to be a lady in those days really wasn't much fun. You had to spend all your time doing embroidery, being respectful to oafish knights, and talking about silly things – you were never allowed to talk about anything serious. Murdina could do all that – she played the game because to have rebelled would have just made life worse – but secretly she dreamed about love, sunshine, blue seas, happy music and sizzling sausages. She had heard that in other countries sausages could sizzle and pop in a pan, rather than float, semi-submerged, in a slowly bubbling, greasy, fatty, glutinous gunge.

So, when Sir Murdure, from far away Almayne, came to visit – with his fancy clothes, confident manner, and gleaming, shiny teeth – she thought he was wonderful. He seemed to be a symbol of all the things she had been dreaming about. She was a teenager now, and he was in his twenties; to her he seemed so mature and masterful.

Her father, however, thought that Sir Murdure was a flashy little twerp, and that Almayne wasn't a very important place.

Now, one of the worst things about being a lady was that your father had you brought up just to have you married off. Some fathers were better than others, but really they never paid much attention to the feelings of their daughters; they just wanted to make connections with other kingdoms and become more powerful.

Murdina's father didn't think much of Sir Murdure as a match for his daughter, but he had heard of another knight, a knight who was definitely looking for a wife. This was Sir Guy, and Sir Guy lived in Southampton, which was nearly as far away as Almayne. Southampton was important because it was a port, and ships from Southampton traded with faraway places such as Genoa, Sicily and Marseilles. Sir Guy's last wife had sadly died of the marsh fever after a visit to Portsmouth, so he needed a new one. Murdina's father thought to himself, 'Aha, if I marry her off to Sir Guy I'll make an important partnership with Southampton, and Southampton is a prosperous city.'

But Murdina had fallen completely in love with Sir Murdure, and they used to sneak out of the castle keep to have a kiss and a cuddle round the back of the bottle dungeon (a very nasty prison with a sloping floor which made it impossible to be comfortable; it was where Murdina's father would put people he didn't like – and that was quite a lot of people).

So when Murdina heard that she was to be married off to Sir Guy, she cried, 'No father, I love Sir Murdure. He is handsome and fit, and he has very shiny teeth – I hear that Sir Guy is old and daft, and for all I know he has false teeth made out of whale bones.'

'You'll do what you're told, young lady,' said her father, who always managed to say things in an annoying and patronising way, 'and as for that flash git, Sir Fancy Pantsy Murdure, he can just bog off back to Almayne.'

So a very resentful and angry Sir Murdure was sent packing, and Murdina was put on a boat that had to sail all the way down the east coast of Scotland and England, turn right at Kent, past Dover, Fairlight and Beachy, then along the south coast to Southampton.

Now that was a very long journey that took several weeks, and Murdina consoled herself by thinking that Southampton was going to be a warmer and sunnier place than her father's castle. She hoped that it would be like the places it traded with – Genoa, Sicily and Marseilles – and that the sky would be blue, and the sea would be blue, and warm breezes would come fluttering in from the Mediterranean.

They approached Southampton at night and at first it did seem to be a beautiful place. There was a castle on a mound, they could see the distant shore of the Isle of Wight (she thought that maybe it was Sicily), and a full moon hung in the sky over the city by the sea.

Well, she married Sir Guy, and that was that. It wasn't so bad at first, it was nice giving picnics and stuff, and being important and having loads of servants; she even had a woman to wash her bum after having a poo. But it wasn't Sicily. The River Itchen was slow and muddy and got its name from all the insects that flew out of its estuary at low tide and made you itchy – the River Test was clearer, but it wasn't exactly blue. The people were slow and dull-witted and always moaning and complaining, and all the town councillors, who Sir Guy had to keep in order, just wanted to prance around and look important.

And as for Sir Guy – well he wasn't that old, and he had all his own teeth, and he was never nasty to her – but he didn't pay her much attention either. He was always doing important things: organising a water supply so that clean water could run down to the city from the springs at Shirley, chairing meetings of the councillors that went on and on and on, entertaining important visitors and looking interested when they made long boring speeches, and riding round the city, looking important himself.

Then Murdina fell pregnant; she felt sick and ill all the way through the pregnancy, and finally gave birth to a baby boy, who they called Bevois. She didn't like him very much, she didn't like babies much anyway, and given that she wasn't happy herself, she had no happiness to share with the baby.

It was then that she started to think about Sir Murdure, with his fashionable clothes and his shiny teeth.

'If I was married to him,' she thought, 'everything would be fine, and I would be happy.'

So Bevois was brought up by nursemaids and servants, and as he grew up he didn't have a lot of contact with his mum; he got his cuddles from his nursemaid, who became his nanny. He ran around the corridors and passages of the castle, and he ranged free through the forest that lay behind Southampton. He grew big and strong. Well – he had a lot more freedom than his mother ever had.

Murdina thought more and more about Sir Murdure, until in her imagination his teeth were even more shiny than ever they really had been, and his face more handsome than ever could be possible. He was her lost love, and when you've got one of those you blow them up into a picture bigger than anything real.

Well, hens hatch eggs, and people who are bored, fed-up and resentful hatch plots – so Murdina hatched a plot. She sent a letter to Sir Murdure in faraway Almayne – and after a few weeks she got a reply: 'Yes, good plan, go for it.'

She then spoke to Sir Guy: 'Husband, we need to go on a tour around Hampshire. Southampton is Hampshire's main city, and you need to show everyone how important you are. You also need to remind some of those minor knights, such as Sir Billy of Basing, and Sir Willy of Winchester, that they owe you money.'

'Wife,' said Sir Guy, 'that's good thinking; we'll set off on Thursday.'

And so they did. They went on a grand tour, and they stayed in very grand places, round and about Hampshire.

It was the eve of Mayday and they were staying in Wherwell Abbey, when Murdina took to her bed, clutching her tummy.

'Oh husband, I'm not well,' she said, 'I think the only thing that will make me feel better is wild boar – I do love a good hog roast.'

'She's having cravings,' thought Sir Guy, 'maybe she's pregnant again. She might give birth to a daughter, and when the girl is old enough I can marry her off to someone even more important than me. Maybe I could even marry her off to King Edgar's son, Ethelred the Unsteady.'

'Righty-ho, wife,' said Sir Guy, 'I'll just nip off into Harewood Forest and do a bit of the old boar hunting. Tonight we'll have a hog roast with gallons of scrumpy cider, and that'll make you feel better.'

Deep in the forest, Sir Guy caught sight of a boar. He whipped up his horse and went chasing after it, but as he entered a clearing in the woods at a place called Deadman's Plack, he found himself facing Sir Murdure and a gang of wicked-looking mercenaries. Mercenaries are soldiers who hire themselves out to the highest bidder, and they really aren't very nice.

'Not good enough, am I?' said Sir Murdure. 'Well, we'll see who's good enough now.'

A massive fight followed. Sir Guy was very brave and very strong, and he killed several of Sir Murdure's mercenaries before he was brought down himself. Then Sir Murdure raised his sword and chopped off Sir Guy's head, and that was the end of him.

Sir Murdure strode into Wherwell Abbey and announced to Murdina: 'Lady, I have a present for you,' and threw a sack at her feet. She opened it up, and there was her husband's head.

'Ooh goody,' she said. 'Let's get married.'

And so it was that they rode back to Southampton at the head of an army of knights, some of whom were Murdure's mercenaries, and some of whom were Sir Guy's knights – those who knew on which side their bread was buttered and thought it best to join the other lot. Well, Sir Murdure was the boss now!

When they came riding through the Bargate, which is the name for the main entrance into the city of Southampton, all the people came out to cheer them. That may not sound very loyal, but the boss is the boss, and if you are one of the ordinary people it is sometimes easier to cheer on whoever it is, and then get on with your own life.

Bevois, however, now he really wasn't happy. He had got on with his dad; they used to go out hawking and boar hunting together, and other such manly pursuits – but now his father's head was dangling from his mother's saddle.

'Mother,' shouted Bevois. 'You rotten pig – how could you do such a wicked thing?'

Well, that really is no way to talk to your mother, even if she does have your dad's head dangling from her saddle; so she got off her horse, and smacked him one round the side of his head, which knocked him over. Bevois ran off to his room, leaving his mother thinking that she was going to have to get rid of him.

So a few days later she summoned a knight called Sir Saba. Now Sir Saba was Sir Guy's brother, and had been in mourning.

'You have to accept that Sir Murdure is the boss round here now,' said Murdina, 'and if you can't accept it I'll have your head too. This is a test of your loyalty. I want you to take Bevois out to the forest, and I want you to kill the little brat. If you do me this favour, I will see that you are well rewarded, and your future here will be assured. I want you to make it look like a hunting accident.'

Sir Saba had no choice – if the Lady Murdina said 'jump', you jumped.

Deep in the forest, with the sun shining through the branches of the trees and making dappled patterns on the ground, Sir Saba drew his sword and faced Bevois.

'I'm sorry Bevois, but you are to die. It is the way of things.'

Bevois looked at Sir Saba, and then got down on his knees and lowered his head.

'Then chop off my head sir, it is a sorry world that I would leave.'

Sir Saba lowered his sword – he knew he couldn't do this terrible thing.

'Come with me Bevois, I keep sheep in the high fields above Portswood village. You must dress as a shepherd, and be a shepherd, and bide your time.'

Then Sir Saba killed a pig, and dipped Bevois' clothes in the blood. He took them back to Southampton and the Lady Murdina as 'proof' that Bevois was dead.

Well, several weeks passed, and as preparations were made for the wedding of Murdina and Murdure, Bevois watched from the high fields above Southampton.

Come the day of the wedding, Bevois stood amongst his sheep and watched the city. He could see the wedding guests streaming in, and flags and banners a-flying, and he could hear the preparations being made for a great feast. When the trumpets sounded it all became too much for him, and he ran down the hill brandishing his shepherd's crook. He went hurtling through the village of Portswood, and then careered down a steep valley, which has ever since been known as Bevois Valley, though it must have had another name then. He charged through the gates of the castle, then crawled underneath the table at which were sitting all the great and important knights, and gave Sir Murdure a massive thwack on the knees with his shepherd's crook.

'Ooooow!' howled Sir Murdure, and ran around the room, bent double and clutching his knees, 'Knights, guards, soldiers – get the little brat.'

All the knights piled in to catch Bevois, and under the table they all got tangled up with each other. Sir Clodwig's boot was in Sir Glodwig's ear, Sir Leodeprance's elbow was in Sir Spareaglance's stomach, and Sir Fladulance's smelly bum was in Sir Gladioli's face. Bevois wriggled out from under this twisting mass of knighthood, and legged it towards the door.

'Oh no you don't,' screamed Murdina, as she came rocketing into the hall like a bat out of hell, and she grabbed Bevois in a neck-lock that had him gasping for breath.

'Sir Saba,' she screeched, 'come here you wretched excuse for a knight.'

'My Lady, My Lady, I could not kill him,' stammered Sir Saba, and in an aside to Bevois he hissed, 'Thanks very much, now that's really dropped me into the doo-doo.'

'This is what you will do, Sir Saba,' snarled Murdina. 'You will take him down to the black and oozy bed of the River Itchen at Northam – just outside the city – and you will bury him up to his neck. You will then let the tide come in and drown him. If you don't do this, it will be you who will be buried up to your neck in the river mud – and I will be happy to watch you drown.'

So a gang of Murdure's mercenaries took Sir Saba and Bevois down to the River Itchen, and the mercenaries watched whilst Saba buried Bevois up to his neck in the mud. They didn't stay to watch him drown because they were missing valuable drinking time at the wedding, and whilst they were not men given to fear, they were terrified that the wedding guests would polish off all the beer, so they went back to the castle, dragging Sir Saba with them.

Poor Bevois; the tide slowly came in, and the water rose till it was over his chin and he thought he'd be drowned for sure. The water was high enough for a ship to come sailing up the central channel, and along came a trading galley from faraway Armenia.

'I think that's someone's head sticking out of the mud,' said one of the sailors (in Armenian).

'Don't be silly,' said another sailor (also in Armenian). 'What sort of person would bury someone up to his neck in mud?' 'These Christians, they're capable of anything,' said the captain. The sailors were all Muslims, and as far as they could see, Christian countries didn't seem to behave in a very Christian manner.

Well, the sailors brought the galley to the very edge of the channel, threw carpets on to the mud, and crawled out to Bevois.

They dug him out using cooking pots and their bare hands.

And that is how Bevois travelled all the way to Armenia (Armenia is landlocked, so they had to walk the last bit). The sailors brought him before their king (who liked a good story) and said, 'Look what we found.'

The king listened to Bevois' story.

'I knew Sir Guy,' he said. 'He was a valiant knight. I want you to stay here and pledge yourself to me as your king. I will have you trained to become one of my knights.'

And so it was that for the next seven years Bevois grew into a young man at the court of King Emryn of Armenia. Now King Emryn had a daughter, and she was called Josian. We know what happens in stories – Josian and Bevois fell in love. At the end of the seven years, on Christmas day, Bevois was riding across the fields on a fine horse. He didn't know it was

Christmas day – how could he? He was at the court of a Muslim king, who held different holy days and different special days. One of King Emryn's men knew that it was Christmas, though. He was a clever man who knew lots of things, but he only used his cleverness to cause trouble.

'Well,' said the knight to Bevois. 'You would ride forth on what is supposed to be your special day, the Feast of the Nativity. Your religion must be pretty useless if you pay it no heed.'

'Oh yeah?' shouted Bevois, who was always quick to anger. 'I'll have you know that I honour this day more than any of the festivals of Mohammed.'

Well, I don't think that either Jesus or Mohammed would think much of this, people fighting in their names, when really all that they're fighting about is their own pride. But, do you know what? Grown-ups are much worse than children, and when grown-ups fight they invent all sorts of excuses, and when they fight over religion they dishonour their religions, because it's really all about themselves.

Bevois and the knight, and the knight's men, set to in a massive scrap, but Bevois was now a powerful warrior: he killed the knight and knocked all his men off their horses.

King Emryn was very cross when he heard about this, and disappointed, because he loved Bevois like a son. He called Bevois to him and said, 'Bevois you dishonour me, and both our religions – you are going to have to go.'

It was Josian who softened the king's heart – she pleaded for Bevois, and she told her father that Bevois could become one of his greatest knights, and that he loved Emryn like a father. Emryn, who was really quite a nice person for a king, relented and said, 'Oh all right; just tell him to behave himself.'

So it was that Bevois become King Emryn's greatest knight. He killed a dragon that was ravaging the kingdom (dragons do that), and he rid the land of thieves and bandits.

But then came some very bad news. King Bradmond of Damascus, a very powerful king, sent a message to King Emryn:

Dear Emryn,

I would like very much to marry your daughter, Josian.

If she were to become my wife I could help you look after your little kingdom in Armenia. We could combine our kingdoms into a federation, and then we could keep things simple by having me as king of both. You could then retire, and live in a nice little flat in the castle gardens.

If you say 'no' to my proposal I will come to Armenia with my very powerful army, lay waste to the whole country with fire and sword, and then knock your block off.

I await a reply at your earliest possible convenience,

Best wishes,
King Bradmond

Well, as you can imagine, that made Emryn very nervous – so he called together a council. A lot of his knights said he should just marry Josian to Bradmond, and accept his fate. It was Josian herself who strode into the council chamber and announced, 'Father, I have a suggestion.'

'Don't come in here,' exclaimed her shocked father, 'this is not a place for females – be a good girl and go back to your embroidery.'

'Father – you must listen,' she shouted.

'No, let her speak,' said one of Emryn's knights. This knight hated the thought of giving up the kingdom to Bradmond, and because he had fought and ridden with Bevois, he had an inkling of what she was about to say.

'Father,' she said before he had time to stop her, 'you know what a great warrior Bevois is. Sometimes the foreigner who has been adopted will fight more fiercely for his new country than someone born and bred there. You have seen Bevois defeat dragons and bandits; now let him lead the army against

Bradmond – if anyone can do the business, it is Bevois.'

Now King Emryn knew that this was true, though he didn't know that the main reason Bevois would want to beat Bradmond was because he was in love with Josian, and the thought that she should be married off to that warlord was unbearable to him.

And so it was that King Emryn knighted Bevois, and it was Sir Bevois that led the army into battle against the mighty army of King Bradmond of Damascus. Bevois had more than his own skill, strength and cunning, however. He also rode a great horse, Arundel, a horse that had been presented to him by Josian herself, and a horse that could be ridden by no one but Josian or Bevois, and he wielded a great sword, Mortglay, that had been forged in the blood of the dragon slain by Bevois, and blessed by the Princess Josian.

You won't be surprised to hear that Sir Bevois was victorious. He proved himself to be a great general, and he returned to Emryn's castle with King Bradmond as a prisoner.

Well, Emryn was a diplomat, and he allowed Bradmond to return to Damascus. He knew that it was best not to cause all sorts of future hatred by being vengeful – but now Bradmond would be beholden to him, so Emryn would be top dog.

Josian was so pleased to see Bevois return in one piece, that when he was stabling Arundel, she came into the stables and fell into his arms. Two other knights saw this, and they ran straight off to King Emryn and told him that his daughter was kissing and cuddling Sir Bevois.

Now Bevois was a great knight. Josian and Bevois loved each other. Maybe that should have pleased King Emryn. But we know that these great kings and knights thought that they owned their daughters, and it was they who chose who their daughters should marry, and given that Emryn had allowed his daughter more freedom than most kings did, this was all too much for him. Emryn's anger was particularly great because he felt that Bevois had betrayed him, and was just taking advantage of Josian. Perhaps, in spite of everything, Emryn still couldn't really see that Josian had a mind of her own.

But Emryn wasn't going to make a scene, he wasn't going to shout at Bevois, or threaten him. Instead he asked him to take a letter to King Bradmond in Damascus. Bevois, of course, didn't know what was written in the letter.

Dear King Bradmond,

I hope you are behaving yourself.

Given that I am now the boss, you must do what I say. However, I don't think you'll mind fulfilling this request, because you have no cause to like the messenger. I would like you, please, on receipt of this letter, to put the bearer thereof, Sir Bevois, to death. I've rather gone off him.

Thank you very much.

Yours faithfully,

Emryn (King)

Well, on receiving this letter, King Bradmond had Bevois flung into a dungeon, a dungeon that just happened to contain two rather venomous dragons. Bevois fought the dragons, but eventually, in the confusion of the fight, the dragons fought each other. Locked together, the dragons poisoned one another. There were times after that when Bevois wished the dragons had killed him, because he was locked in that dungeon for seven long years. He passed the time by writing several books, and composing music. Later on one of the jailers sold the manuscripts to a Viking trader, and he took them to Iceland. They are still there in a little museum in a small town by the sea.

During his time in prison Bevois was mainly fed bran and water, which isn't very nice, or very nourishing. On special days he was given better stuff, vine leaves stuffed with rice and mince, or kebabs with onion and nuts, but that was only on special days, so he grew thinner and thinner.

At the end of the seven years, King Bradmond thought to himself, 'Well, now

Bevois will be weak enough for us to kill him'; and he sent two soldiers down to the dungeon to do Bevois in. Big mistake. Bevois had great reserves of strength – some of this he had inherited from his father, but a lot of it, and he would never admit the fact, was inherited from his mother. He bashed the two soldiers' noggins together, and that was the end of them.

It was night-time, so he crept out of his cell, grabbed the surprised jailer and locked him in with the two dead soldiers, nicked a horse, and galloped off.

When morning came, and it was discovered that Bevois had escaped – you can imagine King Bradmond's rage.

'Catch him – get the rotten twerp – kill him,' shouted Bradmond at his knights, and they all donned their armour and went off in hot pursuit.

Bevois was weak with hunger, so they eventually caught up with him, just as he approached a great castle inhabited by a wicked giant. The giant had heard all about

Bevois and thought to himself, 'If I bash his brains out, King Bradmond will be pleased with me.' So he rushed at Bevois, brandishing his mighty club. Quickly Bevois shouted, 'Aha – my men will bring you down, you great, fetid lump.'

The giant looked at the knights who were following Bevois, and bellowed, 'So these are your men, useless-looking shower of ninnies. I'll bash them first, and then I'll flatten you,' and he proceeded to bash all Bevois' pursuers to bits. Bevois grabbed one of the soldier's swords, and before the giant knew what was happening Bevois had chopped off his head. And that was that. Bevois then went into the castle and had dinner, which made him feel a lot better.

The next morning he set off again – and now he was on a quest (knights like going on quests) and his quest was to find Josian.

On the road he met a palmer. Now, a palmer is a pilgrim, and this man was on his way to Jerusalem – a place that is considered holy by more than one religion, something that meant the people of Jerusalem could flog all sorts of trinkets, but was always bad news when the members of one religion wanted the place exclusively for themselves.

'Ho there, palmer,' said Bevois. 'What is the news? I've been banged up for some years, so I'm out of touch. What of King Emryn, and his daughter Josian?'

'Oh, Princess Josian is married,' replied the palmer. 'She married King Inor.'

Bevois felt a great sinking feeling in his heart.

'She loves this King Inor?' he asked.

'Oh I shouldn't think so,' said the palmer. 'We all know a princess has to do what her dad tells her. They say she loved this bloke called Bevois, but he went back to England. I think he came from some obscure dump called Southampton.'

'Nooooooooo,' cried Bevois, and burst into tears.

'There, there,' said the palmer. 'I didn't expect to see a big tough fellow like yourself get so emotional; what's up mate?'

Bevois told him the whole story.

'Tell you what, mate,' said the palmer, 'I'll swap my special palmer's clothes for your horse, then you can enter Inor's castle dressed as a palmer, suss out what's going on, and no one will know the difference.'

'Nice one,' said Bevois, 'swapsies.'

So they swapped the palmer's clothes for the horse, and the palmer rode on chortling to himself, 'I got a horse for some smelly old rags!'

In those days, castles, whether Muslim or Christian, always welcomed pilgrims, and they had special places where pilgrims could be fed. Sikh temples, or gurdwaras, still do the same thing today – whether they're in England, India, or anywhere else.

So Bevois sat amongst the pilgrims, and it was the Princess Josian herself who brought the food.

'Don't you know me?' said Bevois.

'No, I don't think so,' she replied, 'but you do look a bit familiar.'

'I'm Bevois, Bevois of Southampton.'

'That, sir, is a cruel and foolish thing to say, and anyway, if you were Bevois, I'd whack you one round the ear 'ole, because you disappeared off home.'

'No – I've been in one of King Bradmond's dungeons; your dad wanted me out of the way. I can prove who I am, take me to Arundel the horse.'

Now Arundel was chained up in his stable because he would let no one ride him but Bevois or Josian, and when Bevois saw this he could have cried again. But as soon as Bevois entered the stable, Arundel whinnied, reared up, and broke his chains – and Josian knew that it really was Bevois.

'I love you, Bevois,' she shouted, 'and I really don't like King Inor. He is old and smelly, and won't stop blowing off really stinky ones – let us fly from here.'

And so they both leaped astride Arundel and galloped away, though not before seizing the mighty sword Mortglay.

Well, they were long gone before anyone knew, and Arundel was the fastest horse in the land, so Inor had little chance of catching them. There were plenty of other dangers to face, though.

As they rode down a rocky track through wild mountains, a mighty giant stepped in front of them. He was covered in bristles like a wild boar, and he snorted and grunted.

'Not another one,' thought Bevois.

'Ho there,' boomed the giant. 'I am the mighty Ascupart, and this is my valley – Ascupart Valley. No one passes this way without a scrap.'

'One day,' thought Bevois, 'I'm going to have a valley named after me, and maybe it too will be a dodgy place, but for now – I must battle this giant.'

Bevois dismounted, and drew his great, shining sword, Mortglay. The two of them set to in a mighty battle. The giant wielded his club, but Bevois was faster, though Mortglay wasn't exactly a small sword. After fighting for three days the two of them were exhausted, and Josian was really quite bored with watching them. Bevois and Ascupart both fell on to their backs, and Josian poured some of their precious water over Bevois' face. 'Now's your chance,' she whispered.

Bevois, dragging his sword, staggered across to Ascupart, and lifted the mighty Mortglay, ready to chop off the giant's head.

'That's enough,' shouted Josian. 'You don't have to actually kill him. Spare him and let him come with us, he'll be handy in a fight.'

'Lady,' said Bevois, feeling a bit miffed, 'he may betray us.'

'Listen, Bevois, I gave you that sword, and I'm saying don't kill him.'

'I'll second that,' said Ascupart from the ground. 'You really wouldn't want to upset the lady. Spare me, and I'll be true to you.'

'Then rise, and live,' announced Bevois rather grandly, whilst Josian raised her eyes to the sky – like you do when someone is being a bit of a fancy-pants.

So off they went, until they came to the Mediterranean Sea. There was a ship in port, and Ascupart shouted, 'Ahoy there, mateys, have you got room for a lady, a bloke, a horse, and – um – a giant?'

'Only if you've got the money,' the captain shouted back.

'I've got a few quid,' bellowed the giant. 'Send us a boat.'

'Not likely,' shouted the captain. 'I don't like the look of you.'

So Ascupart picked up Arundel, and put him under one arm, then he picked up Josian and Bevois and put them under the other arm, and waded out to the ship.

'You'd better take us,' said Ascupart to the captain, 'or it'll be the worse for you'.

'Um, all right then. We're going to Venice.'

'Oooh, that's nice,' said Bevois, 'I've always wanted to go to Venice. We can then have a walk across the mountains and go and see my uncle, who is Archbishop of Cologne. It's rather a long walk, but it should be very scenic, and no doubt we can have a few adventures on the way.'

And that's just what they did.

Well, after a lot of adventures, they eventually arrived in Cologne, and Bevois' uncle said, 'You two had better get married, you obviously love each other, and people are going to get a bit cross if you hang around together all this time without being married. That sort of thing might have been all right in classical antiquity, but it's the Middle Ages now, and we're much more modern.'

'Ah,' said Josian, 'that is a little bit of a problem – I already am married.'

'*WHAT*? Aaargh! That really is very naughty,' shrieked the Archbishop of Cologne, 'Who are you married to?'

'King Inor.'

'Ah – you're a Muslim then?'

'Yes, indeed I am.'

Now, neither Muslims nor Christians took a lot of time out to examine what their religions really meant, and neither respected the other's marriage vows.

'If you become a Christian,' said the archbishop, thinking he could add another name to his list, 'we won't count your marriage to King Inor, and you can marry my nephew.'

Well, Josian didn't like the idea – it felt like a betrayal of everything she was brought up with. But then she thought about her father marrying her off to someone she didn't love, of how he'd tricked Bevois, and about how it was really all about these blokes and their endless politics, and nothing really about religion at all.

'It wouldn't make any difference if I was Muslim, Christian, Jewish, Hindu, Buddhist, Zoroastrian, or whatever religion those doddery old druids I keep falling over in the forests have,' she thought. 'Really, it's all just words: like stories.'

So she agreed to become a Christian.

Then the archbishop turned to Ascupart the giant.

'You too must be baptised a Christian,' he said, 'and we have built an especially large font to christen you in.'

'You can get stuffed,' roared Ascupart, 'I'm not becoming a Christian for no one,' and he picked up the font and dropped it over the archbishop's head. They could all hear the archbishop shouting from inside the font: 'Let me out, let me out!'

'It'll take a while for all the priests and monks to get him out of that,' said Bevois – and turning to Josian, he said, 'Let's get wed in Southampton, in Saint Michael's Church – but this means I've got some business to attend to.'

So, accompanied by many soldiers from Cologne, they set off for England. Before they left the soldiers sprinkled themselves with holy water from Cologne Cathedral, which meant that Bevois' army was known as the Eau de Cologne.

They travelled west to the coast of France, from whence they took a ship to the Isle of Wight.

On the Isle of Wight, whom should they find but Sir Saba.

'Ever since I refused to kill you, Bevois, the Lady Murdina and Sir Murdure have turned against me. They heard that you were alive in the East, and they vowed to kill me. So I fled to Wight, and I have many trusty men with me. Southampton has become a tyranny; they have built a mighty stadium for terrible sacrificial sports, and have invited in Scandinavian mercenaries to build great market places in which the citizens are forced to buy the most useless goods, and so many have fled across to the Island.'

And so it was that the Eau de Cologne gang joined the Island crew, and they all sailed to Southampton and attacked the surprised Sir Murdure.

There was a massive battle. It ranged from the village of Sholing across to the village of Millbrook, over the sea to the Isle of Wight, and back again. Finally, in the midst of battle, Ascupart the giant caught hold of Sir Murdure, and hurled him into a spiky hedge to the east of Southampton. That is where Sir Murdure met his end – which is why the place of Sir Murdure's death has ever since been known as Hedge End.

As for Murdina – she let out a terrible scream and threw herself into a deep, dark pool, a terrible place full of water dragons and monsters, known as Shirley Pond. The water sizzled and steamed as she sank beneath the surface, and continued boiling and bubbling until it was cooled by ice from a place nearby, known as the Ice House.

And so it was that Bevois returned to Southampton, and Bevois and Josian ruled Southampton, and it is said that they ruled wisely and well.

Hundreds of years ago everyone knew stories about Sir Bevois. They wouldn't always be the same – everyone had their own versions, and no doubt everyone thought that their own version was the 'proper' one. Shakespeare, in the play *Henry VIII*, when describing a fabulous scene, said that it was so impressive that you'd almost believe 'that former fabulous story' about Bevis (who in Southampton is known as Bevois). So these stories were known to be great exaggerations used by the common people.

Southampton laid particular claim to these stories, possibly because of the popularity of a fourteenth-century written romance called *Bevis of Hampton*, Hampton being the old name for Southampton. Mind you, there was an ancient monument called Bevis's Grave on top of Portsdown Hill, overlooking Portsmouth, and another in Arundel in Sussex (same name as the horse), and another ancient monument called Bevis's Thumb, near the Hampshire-Sussex border at Compton. I guess that there was a much older story that just got adapted by the writer in the fourteenth century, just as I've adapted it now – though that fourteenth-century romance is my main source.

Another ancient monument, called Bevis's Tomb, was on top of a hill called Bevois Mount, then just outside Southampton. This got swallowed up by buildings as the city expanded. But the Bevois story is there in the place names of Southampton. There is an area of town called Bevois Town (with a school called Bevois Town Primary School), there is a road called Bevois Valley; and this is all around the hill that, before it all got built on, was known as Bevois Mount.

There is a street called Ascupart Street, and an old tower called Arundel Tower – though it can be a bit draughty at times, so people sometimes call it Catchecold Tower.

In the middle of Southampton there is an old gateway called the Bargate – it was the medieval entrance to the city – and in it there are two old paintings, one of Bevois, and one of Ascupart. I love the fact that even though people have forgotten the stories, the names are still there in the fabric of Southampton.

The sword Mortglay, however, is not in Southampton; it is in Arundel Castle in Sussex. I reckon that they nicked it, and that the people of Southampton should all march to Arundel Castle and demand it back.

5

THE
DISMAL
DANES

PART ONE
THE DANESTREAM

The Danes figure quite a lot in the folk tales of Hampshire. The Danes were Vikings, and they spent much of the ninth century raiding the Saxon kingdom of Wessex. What is now England was then comprised of different countries, and Hampshire was not only part of Wessex, but contained the capital, Winchester. During this time the Danes were busy setting up their own country in England; a great slice of land stretching from what is now Cumbria in the north-west, right down to the east coast as far as London. This country was called the Danelaw.

I wonder, sometimes, if some of those old dragon stories are really about the Vikings, because didn't the Vikings have dragon heads carved on the prows of their longships? In a lot of folk tales the dragons guarded hoards of treasure, and not only did the Vikings love plundering for treasure, the Saxons would often have to give them treasure to buy them off – please, take the money and go away!

Whether that's true or not, I don't know – but I do know a story about a stream called the Danestream, and that the story has got a dragon in it.

The Danestream is located at the south-western corner of the New Forest; it rises at a place called Bashley, after which it flows down a valley between the villages of Ashley and Hordle, then out to sea at Millford.

I do love the names of these villages in the south-west of the New Forest:

> Bashley, Ashley,
> Tiptoe, Hordle,
> Boldre, Bransgore,
> Burley and Sway.

If you say them out loud, it's a poem!

It is said that sometimes the water of the Danestream runs red – and the reason given isn't because of red soil, but because it flows with the blood from a great battle that took place near Bashley. I don't know about that – but here's the story:

Once upon a time a great dragon came to the village of Bashley, and ravaged the surrounding countryside. We have already seen that dragons were rather fond of ravaging, and that no one can go out and farm the land and generally earn a decent living whilst dragons are thundering around the place, burning the crops and flame-grilling the cattle.

So the people called out to the king to come and help them, and the king was none other than Alfred the Great, and he had his court in Winchester.

So King Alfred girded on his sword, mounted his great steed, and rode down to Bashley, ready to do battle with the fearsome dragon. The dragon roared, the king shouted his battle cry, they charged at each other, and the king sliced off the dragon's head. The trouble was, though, that after Alfred chopped the dragon's head off, it grew two more – and when he chopped them off, it grew four more, and then it was eight, and then sixteen, and so on, with the king's sword arm getting more and more tired.

Well, the battle wasn't going well for Alfred – but then he remembered something that he'd heard a long time before. It was from a time when he'd been on the run from the Danes, those vile Vikings, and he'd been hiding out in a marshy place called the Somerset Levels. He had been staying with an old woman, and when she'd asked him to look after her cakes that were baking in the hearth, whilst she went out to milk the cow, he had let them burn. This was because he was a lousy cook; being a king he had always had servants to cook the food. This had made her really cross, and I don't blame her. 'If I wasn't an old woman,' she had shouted, 'I'd throw you into running water, and watch you being washed away like a dragon.'

'Running water,' thought Alfred. 'Dragons hate running water.' So, just as the dragon was busy growing sixty-four heads, Alfred charged at it; and he and his mighty steed pushed the dragon into the stream. It immediately shrivelled up, and was washed away down the river. Some say that it was washed all the way out to the sea at Millford; but others say that it crawled out of the stream at the place that was later to be called Hordle, because that was where it kept its treasure, and it sleeps there still – under the hill, which is now under the village.

So it is that the river runs red with dragon blood (Alfred threw all the heads into the water) and Hordle got its name because beneath it lies a dragon hoard. There is a hill there called Golden Hill, which is named after the treasure, and the fumes from the dragon's breath seep up through the soil, which explains why the inhabitants of Hordle are a bit weird. Oh – and Bashley is called Bashley because that is where King Alfred bashed the dragon.

Maybe, though, the dragon really represents the Danes, and there was a battle between the Saxons of Wessex and the Viking Danes; the Danes were defeated, and the stream ran red with their blood. That would explain the name.

I did read somewhere, however, that the 'Dane' in the word 'Danestream' comes from an old Saxon word *Denu*, which means 'stream'. But then that would mean that Danestream means 'Streamstream', so I like my story better! And what is more, I looked up the name 'Hordle' in my great big book of English place names, and it says that the word probably comes from the Old English words *hord-hyll*, which means 'treasure mound' – so maybe the story is true after all.

PART TWO
GUY AND COLBRAND

The terrible time when the Danes were attacking the country, when no one was able to feel safe, stayed in the memory of the people through the stories. In medieval times,

500 years later, the stories were transformed into tales of knights in armour. One of these stories was about a knight called Guy of Warwick and was popular in Hampshire as well as Warwickshire because it told of a great battle near Winchester.

But – to begin at the beginning. Guy was a mighty knight who lived in Warwick, and who spent a great deal of time clobbering anyone who was considered an enemy. This made him a very great man in the eyes of a lot of people – but still, when he fell in love with Felice the Fair, daughter of Roland, Earl of Warwick, he wasn't considered posh enough for the daughter of an earl.

This meant he had to go off and prove himself – so off he went to the country of his enemies, which was possibly the Danelaw. Now, this was in the days when Athelstan was king, and Warwick was on the very edge of the Danelaw. So Guy did lots of bashing and thrashing, and built himself up an even greater reputation as an almighty hero. Then he went back home, and found that he was expected to do still more bashing in order to prove himself worthy of Felice the Fair.

So he had to fight a dragon – isn't that always the case? Then he had to fight a particularly fierce wild boar, and we've already seen that there's lots of them about too. Then he had to fight a giant cow. I'm not joking – it was called the Dun Cow. 'Dun' means 'brown'. Fight a brown cow? How now, brown cow. This cow was huge, the size of an elephant, and it was terrorising the neighbourhood. Maybe there is some more meaning behind all this. Throughout England there are pubs called 'The Dun Cow' – believe me, I've been in a few of them, so there would seem to be a history here, and sometimes people like to call beer 'the milk of the Dun Cow'. A nineteenth-century writer called Isaac Taylor suggested that the phrase 'Dena Gau' has changed over the centuries, so it sounds like 'Dun Cow', and that the phrase 'Dena Gau' means 'The Danish Region'. So perhaps Guy was really fighting the Danes, in a region near Warwick.

Anyhow, at this stage Roland, Earl of Warwick, died, and at last Guy was allowed to marry Felice, though I don't know what she thought about this, and he became Sir Guy, Earl of Warwick.

He'd achieved his aim – hooray – so shouldn't this be the end of the story? And shouldn't this story be in a book of Warwickshire folk tales?

It is a terrible fact, though, that when great, long-sought after goals are achieved, then it all turns to ashes.

Sir Guy of Warwick was sick at heart. He'd fought dragons, wild boars and giant cows. He had fought Danes. Lots of them. Lots of battles. Lots of killing. Lots of horrors. He sat on his great chair in Warwick Castle, and wondered if it was all worth it. He lost his appetite, he didn't want to quaff ale (and when a great lord was off his ale that was serious) and he felt no pleasure in the company of Felice, though he loved her well.

Time for a pilgrimage.

He put aside his sword, hung his armour up in the wardrobe, and donned the cloak of a pilgrim. He fixed a cockleshell, the symbol of a pilgrim, to his cloak, cut himself a stout staff – and set off for the Holy Land.

Felice also gave herself up to religious practice. She sold her jewels and her fine clothes, she gave money to the poor, she built homes for orphans and widows, and she built a large hospital. To be honest, she was being a lot more useful than Sir Guy, but everyone to their own way. I don't know if she managed to rule Warwick as well – maybe she employed an estate agent.

Well, Sir Guy was gone for a long time; his hair turned white, his beard grew all the way down to his belly, and his clothes were in rags. He became very holy, and entirely turned his back on bashing and thrashing, which seems to me like a good thing. However – sometimes things come back to haunt you.

One day, when Sir Guy was far away in the East, he came upon a graveyard. Lying in the graveyard there was a worm-eaten skull.

Sir Guy picked up the worm-eaten skull and spoke to it (pilgrims do this sort of thing):

'Perhaps you were a prince or a mighty monarch, a king, a duke, or a lord. But king or beggarman, we all return to the earth. Perhaps you were a queen, or a duchess, or some such high-born lady, but queen or washerwoman, we all end up being eaten by the worms.'

'Blimey,' said the skull. 'If I had a penny for every time someone picked me up and came out with all that old guff, there'd be a pile of treasure here.'

To say that Sir Guy was a bit startled would be an understatement. He dropped the skull.

'Oy, pick me up, Sir Pilgrim,' ordered the skull. 'I've got something important to tell you.'

Sir Guy picked the skull up, keeping his fingers well clear of the gnashing teeth.

'Whilst you've been wandering around thinking about your almighty soul,' said the skull, in a very disrespectful manner, 'Wessex has been suffering mightily. The Danes have never left off their raiding, so no one has been able to safely work the fields and grow their crops; they've all been living in fear and hunger. You know what happens when the Danes turn up – same thing every time, they've got no imagination; they steal the treasure, burn the village, church, monastery or priory, and kill the people or take them as slaves. The people have been living in a state of constant anxiety, fearful that they might see a line of those stupid-looking helmets, and then find themselves set upon by another horde of vile Vikings. Worse still, some of these Vikings have managed to leave off bashing each other long enough to join together and form an army, and this army has invaded Wessex.'

'Alas, poor Warwick, I know it well,' howled Sir Guy to the skull.

'Never mind Warwick,' said the skull, 'this is a book of Hampshire folk tales, and the Viking army is besieging Winchester, and King Athelstan is holed up inside.'

So it was that Sir Guy of Warwick knew it was time to return. Bringing the skull with him, he took ship on a galley carrying barrels of wine bound for Southampton, and then took the old pathway along the River Itchen. Sir Guy came to a ridge overlooking Winchester (a ridge that is now called Oliver's Battery after Oliver Cromwell, and a later war, and a later siege), and there he saw the mighty army of Danes camped around the city walls, just sitting, waiting for the citizens of Winchester to run out of food and surrender. Athelstan didn't want to surrender, he was well aware of the horrors that would be unleashed if he did, and the Danes would certainly do something very nasty to him.

Sneaking through the Viking army wasn't easy, but when one Dane saw him, Sir Guy held up the skull, which chattered its teeth, and said something very rude.

'Aaargh, Sköll!' screamed the Viking, and fled. (Sköll is a kind of Viking demon.) He didn't tell any other Vikings, because Vikings aren't allowed to admit to running away, so Sir Guy was able to sneak on through.

He found a small door in the city wall; it was at the back – a tucked away part of town called Winnall. He held the skull up to the grid on the door, and it clattered its teeth, stared at the guard and mesmerised him.

'Open the door,' ordered the skull.

So it was that Sir Guy, dressed as a pilgrim, entered Winchester, and presented himself before the king. He regaled the king with tales of the Holy Land, and the latest news from Francia, whilst the skull sang a few folk songs, and for a while King Athelstan was able to forget the horrors that beset him.

But the next morning there came a terrible roar from the Viking army. They started to shout, and banged their swords on their round shields. The men of Wessex watched from the city walls as a huge and terrible giant stepped forward from the ranks of the Danes. He had a massive black beard, very sinister-looking eye make-up, and he was brandishing an enormous, wooden club.

'*I AM COLBRAND*,' he roared in a voice as deep as thunder, 'and you Wessexonians are a bunch of cowards. You boast of your great deeds in the stories, but you are nothing but a bunch of foxes that hide in the woods. You are a trembling bunch of plucked chickens, and you all smell of poo. Send me forth your champion – I challenge him to single combat.'

Well, several knights did go to King Athelstan and offer to be his champion, though all of them knew that they didn't stand a chance. To the king, however, the strangest offer came from the old, white-haired pilgrim.

'I had foresworn violence,' he said, 'but now I know there is no choice. I will be your champion.'

'What foolishness is this?' said the king, but there was something about the tall pilgrim that stopped him from dismissing the whole idea. 'We have no armour for one as tall as you,' he said.

'Send word to Warwick, I would have Guy of Warwick's armour.'

'Guy of Warwick is long gone. They say he went mad and disappeared to foreign lands. After the Danes have taken Winchester, they will surely go north and take Warwick.'

'Send for the armour, My Lord. If the Lady Felice is given this pilgrim shell, she will know to send it.'

Well, a soldier went to the battlements, and shouted, 'Hang on, lads, give us a few days, and we'll find someone to fight your giant.'

The Danes fell about laughing.

'Ooooh, give us a few days,' they mocked in silly voices.

'You have a few days,' roared Colbrand. 'A few days to say your prayers, before I slay your champion.'

So, a scout was sent out through the Winnall door, and he took the skull, which helped him sneak through the Viking lines. He got himself a horse in the village of King's Worthy, and galloped all the way to Warwick. When the Lady Felice saw the pilgrim shell, she knew that Sir Guy was back.

The scout returned to Winchester, capital of Wessex, and once again sneaked through the Viking lines – no mean feat whilst carrying a large bag full of armour. He was, of course, aided by the skull, which did seem to make Danes run away on an individual basis, and maybe the Vikings were so used to victory, and the terror of their victims, that they were careless; they never felt that they were ever in any danger.

The scout, and the bag full of armour, was admitted through the Winnall door, and everyone, including Athelstan, looked on in amazement as the armour was seen to fit the pilgrim perfectly. Probably, they started to guess who he was.

So, the pilgrim, clad in shining armour, strode out of the main gates of Winchester to face the giant Colbrand. The Danes roared and banged their shields – and up they all went to a place called Norn Hill, where the fight was to take place.

A Dane strode forward and rang a bell.

'Seconds away, round one,' he shouted, and the two fighters began their battle, each knowing that there was only going to be one round, a long one, and only one end, a death.

Back in Winchester the skull snapped its teeth, and suddenly grew wings. 'Craak,' it croaked as it changed into a terrible, gaunt-looking crow and flapped its way towards Norn Hill.

The fight lasted for hours. Sir Guy, even though he wasn't as young as he used to be, was the faster of the two, but, tall as he was, he looked like a dwarf next to the giant Colbrand. A strange crow, however, came 'craaaking' out of the sky and flew around the giant's head, continually bothering and bedizening him.

Every swing of Sir Guy's sword seemed to take a slice off the giant's great, wooden club, and it got smaller, and smaller, and smaller, whilst the crow croaked in the giant's ear every time he tried to bash Sir Guy. This went on until the giant, meaning to take a great swipe at Sir Guy, realised that all that was left of his club was a little splinter of wood, the size of a toothpick.

'Oh,' he said in astonishment, and stopped and gazed at the toothpick. Sir Guy moved in close, and chopped off the giant's head.

'*I AM THE VICTOR!*' Sir Guy bellowed at the Danes. '*TURN NOW AND LEAVE THIS PLACE.*'

'*CRAAAK,*' said the crow.

By all the rules, that was what they were supposed to do – but never trust a Viking.

'*KILL HIM!*' shouted their leader. '*AND TAKE WINCHESTER BEFORE THE FOOLS SHUT THE GATE.*'

At that moment there came a terrible shriek from up on Chilcomb Down (Downs are always up) – and a shriek can be more terrifying and blood-freezing than the deepest of shouts. Up on the hill, mounted on a great white horse, was the Lady Felice, and the horse reared, before galloping down the slope towards the Danes. Behind her, with a roar, came the army of Warwick.

Or at least, half the army of Warwick, because from Magdalene Hill Down, on the other side of the valley, came the other half. Then, from out of the gates of Winchester galloped Athelstan's men, and the Danes, caught between the three charging hordes, were annihilated.

So, Wessex was saved from the Danes, and after feasting and rejoicing, and rewards from King Athelstan, Felice, Guy, the skull (no longer a crow), and the men of Warwick took their leave.

It is said that Sir Guy never took up his place as Earl of Warwick, sitting on his great chair in Warwick Castle. He'd doubly had enough of war and bloodshed, and finally thought that, in the woods and fields of his homeland, his pilgrimage was really over. It is also said that he went to live in a cave near Warwick, whilst the skull sat outside shouting very rude things at unwelcome visitors.

Maybe it was the Lady Felice who continued to rule Warwick wisely and well, or maybe she

left it to the estate agent. That I don't know –
I'd think I'd better leave that to the author of a
book about Warwickshire folk tales to tell us.

PART THREE
SAINT SWITHUN AND THE EGGS

These stories describing the effect the Danes
had on Wessex are full of fighting and violence,
and that is not surprising. There is one story,
though, that feels quite different – it is about
a gentle man, and an act of kindness.

We don't really know much about
Swithun, except that he became Bishop
of Winchester in 852. Stories have grown
around him, though, and one of these can
be seen pictured on the wall of a little Saxon
church in the village of Corhampton, in the
Meon Valley. Once upon a time the walls of
most churches were covered in paintings –
and almost like a comic strip or a graphic
novel, these were paintings that told stories.
During a time called the Reformation, in the
sixteenth century, most of these paintings

were destroyed – sometimes they were gouged out of the walls, sometimes they were whitewashed over. In 1968 some of the old paintings were discovered beneath the whitewash in Corhampton Church (you can see them now), and one of them tells the story of Swithun and the eggs.

Swithun had ordered that a bridge should be built over the River Itchen, at the bottom of Winchester High Street. When the building was finished, Swithun blessed the bridge, and then stood on it to preach a sermon to the crowd. But this was the time when the Danes were constantly attacking and raiding Wessex, and the people had developed the bad manners and lack of care of people who lived in a dangerous time, a time when people learned to look after themselves before others.

In the crowd there was an old woman carrying a basket of eggs that she planned to sell at the market. She was pushed and jostled by the crowd, until she dropped the basket and all the eggs were broken.

As she scrabbled around after the basket, the people continued to jostle the old woman, and she would surely have been trampled underfoot if there hadn't been a great roar from the bridge. '*SILENCE!*' shouted Swithun. 'Have you fools no care?'

Swithun strode through the crowd to the old woman, and helped her to her feet. He then knelt down and gathered up the fragments of eggshell, and as he did so, the eggs were miraculously restored, and it was a basket of whole eggs that he handed back to the woman.

This is a little story, but it is good to have a story that represents an act of humanity and kindness in a troubled time.

Before Swithun died it is said that he made it clear that he didn't want to be buried in Winchester Cathedral, but outside, where the rain would fall on his grave. The monks didn't think it was right that the Bishop of Winchester should be buried outside, so they buried the body in an ornate crypt inside the cathedral. Saint Swithun was so cross, that he caused the rain to pour down in torrents, and the people were in danger of losing the harvest. So they buried the body outside after all, and the rain stopped, the sun came out, and the birds sang in the trees.

Since then it has been said that if it rains on Saint Swithun's Day, which is the 15th July, it will rain for forty days after, which will be very bad for the harvest.

Saint Swithun's Day if thou dost rain,
For forty days it will remain.
Saint Swithun's Day if thou be fair,
For forty days 'twill rain no more.

6

THE PLAGUE

PART ONE
THE VICAR OF VERNHAM DEAN

Before the twentieth century, London must have seemed a long way away from Hampshire, but the presence of this great city, lurking just over the horizon, was still strongly felt. The nineteenth-century writer and traveller, William Cobbett, called London 'the great wen', and the word 'wen' means 'cyst', or puss-filled spot. People in the countryside often thought of London as a wen, or as a great big steaming gone-off stew. So when the plague hit London, there was always great fear in Hampshire, and a great suspicion of strangers, strangers who might be escaping from London Town, and who might be infected.

Such a stranger may have passed through the village of Vernham Dean, a village that nestles in a valley, amidst the high downland hills of north-west Hampshire, hills that stretch into Berkshire and Wiltshire.

The plague took root in Vernham Dean, and the vicar was overcome by horror.

'What to do? What to do?'

The vicar realised that he was the person who had to decide; the responsibility fell upon his shoulders.

He knew the story of Eyam in Derbyshire – in Eyam the plague-stricken villagers had cut off all access to the outside world to avoid infecting anyone else, and so they had all died together. Surely, Vernham Dean could do the same. But the vicar didn't have the plague himself, and he was terrified of it. Well, who wouldn't be? The thought of those horrible swelling buboes appearing in his armpits was beyond description.

So he took the villagers up the hill, to a remote and lonely track called Chute Causeway – an ancient Roman Road that, unusually for a Roman Road, curves around the hill – way up on the high wind-blown slopes of the Downs. There, next to Chute Causeway, by Tidcombe Long Barrow, they set up camp.

The vicar, however, didn't stay with them. There was no source of water up on the hill, and the villagers would need food, so the vicar said, 'I'll bring you up food and water, I'll keep you supplied.'

… and he really meant it. He wasn't trying to deceive them, he really intended to toil up the hill and bring them provisions on a regular basis.

But when he was back down in Vernham Dean, he looked up at that hill – and he thought of all those plague-stricken people, and of how they might infect him, and he shivered with disgust and trembled with fear. He knelt in the church and prayed for them, but it didn't do them much good. Up by Tidcombe Long Barrow, the villagers died of thirst and hunger, and, of course, the plague.

But the vicar himself had already contracted the disease, and so he too died, down in the village, and there was no one to look after him.

It is said that ever since then, should you be walking Chute Causeway on a moonlit night, you might see the ghost of the vicar of Vernham Dean, trying to bring food and water up to the plague-stricken villagers, but he can never quite make it far enough.

Oh dear – that's not a very nice story, but then the plague wasn't very nice. I'm glad of all those developments in medicine and hygiene that have made the plague a thing of the past.

PART TWO
THE PLAGUE TREASURE OF PRESTON CANDOVER

In another part of Hampshire, in a village called Preston Candover (we do like our villages to have two-word names!), everyone was horror struck when a plague victim arrived from London Town.

He arrived on horseback, and was far gone with the plague. The horse had bags full of money dangling from it; the man had taken as much of his fortune as he could – not knowing when he escaped the plague-ridden cesspit that was London Town that he'd already contracted the disease himself. Leaning forward on his poor old horse, as it hobbled through Preston Candover, the man died.

The villagers stood around horse and corpse, at a safe distance, and wondered what to do. They were poor people and they wanted that money, but their terror of the plague was stronger than their desire for riches, so they shot the poor horse, dug a great hole, and pushed horse, man and treasure into it, before filling it in.

There then grew up a story about buried treasure in Preston Candover, and the books about Hampshire legends tell us that 'neither treasure nor bones have ever been discovered'. But then, if no one knows where the treasure was buried, how do they know that no one has discovered it?

You see, someone did take it – but that leads to another story, and I need to start that story at the beginning, because it is silly to start a story at the end – that would mean telling it backwards. Before I start the story, though, I need to tell you about the Hampshire fairisies.

PART THREE
THE HAMPSHIRE FAIRISIES

Hampshire people don't talk with that old, strong, country accent any more, but when they did people in both Hampshire and the neighbouring county of Sussex would use something called 'the reduplicating plural'.

To use the plural means to talk about more than one. So, we can talk about one fairy, or two fairies. In Hampshire and Sussex, however, they'd say that plural twice, so they'd say 'two fairisies'. When learned people came down from London to study folklore, and they wrote down dialect words in their special, leather-bound folklore collecting notebooks, they wrote down the word 'fairisies' as 'Pharisees'. This caused endless confusion, because the Pharisees are a group of people in the bible, and when the vicar stood in his pulpit, giving a sermon, people didn't know if he was talking about a religious sect in Biblical times or the local fairies.

Anyhow, most English counties have particular areas that are favourite places for the fairisies – and in Hampshire it is the area around the town of Liphook, close to the border with Sussex, an area of woods, hedgerows, fields and low rolling hills. The fairisies are not often spotted nowadays because they hate road traffic, so you'll never see them from the roads, but if you walk the paths, tracks and green lanes, you might occasionally get a glimpse of them. You only ever see them out of the corner of your eye, never directly – well that is except for a few special people. These people see the whole countryside light up and they get to see the other world, and all the fairisies going about their business. I've never had that experience myself; the one time I thought I had, it turned out that I was accidentally trespassing on the grounds of a conference centre, or some such place, and so all the intruder deterrent lights had turned on. The security man wasn't at all happy when I said that I thought it was the fairisies.

If you are one of the few unusual enough to see the fairisies, you will see that they are not the little winged, dainty creatures from

Disney films, but that they come in all shapes and sizes, and some of them can be quite scary. They can also take the form of animals; one of these, often seen around Liphook, takes the form of a little white calf. If you follow it down the road, and the road crosses running water, the calf will shrink till it is just the size of a cockerel, and then – 'pop' – it vanishes.

But then the fairisies delight in doing odd things – and another of the fairisies in that area takes the form of a little boy who can play beautiful music on a little flute. And this leads me to the story that I was going to tell.

PART FOUR
THE SHINING CITY

Once upon a time there was a preacher, and he had been preaching the gospel in Liphook, and was riding north-westwards towards Alton.

Firstly he saw the fairy calf, but as he thought that belief in the fairisies was sinful, he tried to ignore it. It ran in front of him along the green way, until it disappeared whilst crossing the River Wey. Whilst he was recovering from this strange experience, he heard the sound of a flute, and it was the most enchanting music he had ever heard. There, just ahead, and a little to one side of his horse, was a boy, skipping along and playing the flute.

The preacher called out to the boy, but got no answer. He had the distinct impression that the boy wanted him to follow, and so, like the Pied Piper in reverse, the preacher followed the child.

They went uphill and down dale, across fields and along remote tracks, through wild woodland and open heathland, for mile after mile, until the preacher had travelled a whole day and a whole night. Early in the morning the preacher found himself by some gravel pits near Preston Candover. As he looked at the little musician, the boy shrank and disappeared, just like the fairy calf had done.

The preacher realised that there was something special about the place where the fairy boy had disappeared, so he marked the spot, and returned the following day with a spade.

Well, he worked hard, and he dug and he dug, until he came across the bones of a

human and a horse, lying where they had been buried by the villagers of Preston Candover two centuries before. Lying amidst the bones and the gravel were bags of gold coins, now surely free of the plague.

His next problem was what to do with them. He was a preacher, a man of God. He felt that the gold was a gift from God, even though he had been led there by the fairisies, and he thought about the Golden City. He knew his bible well, and in the Book of Revelations, in the New Testament, the bible speaks of a city of gold – and long had he dreamed of this celestial city.

So he invested the money, and then he married a rich merchant's daughter from Mapledurwell, and he passed the dream on to his son. It was several generations before the dream was realised. His descendants were instrumental in using this money to build a real golden city, a wondrous and marvellous place: Basingstoke.

Some people call Basingstoke doughnut city, because it has so many roundabouts, and indeed it is a place where drivers can very easily get lost – they say that there is one Morris Minor that has been driving around since 1969 looking for a way out.

However, the town of Basingstoke wouldn't exist if it hadn't been for the preacher, and the preacher would have never found the gold if it hadn't of been for the fairisies, and the gold would never have been there if it hadn't of been for the plague, spilling out of London Town. So Basingstoke is built upon London's overspill.

7

THE
BLACKSMITH
OF TWYFORD

PART ONE
THE FATHER OF THE CRAFTSMEN

The blacksmith always used to be a very important person in a community – and yet, somehow, a little bit disapproved of. People tended to be scared of him, this rough man in his forge of fire, sparks, and ringing, metallic noises.

Maybe this goes right back to the Iron Age – when metal was newly discovered, and the smith was creating new materials of incredible strength and power, so he might be viewed as a god or a devil. Of course the smith could be making objects that can be used for evil or good: swords or ploughshares.

Perhaps the story of Arthur pulling the sword from the stone goes right back to the process of casting a sword blade – whereby white-hot liquid metal is poured into a stone mould – and when the cooled blade is drawn from the stone, it looks almost magical. If King Arthur did draw the sword, Excalibur, from a stone, it must surely have been in Hampshire, because Arthur's round table hangs in the great hall in Winchester, and that means Winchester must be the site of Arthur's legendary court, Camelot. I would say that, of course, because I live in Hampshire – really there are lots of places that claim King Arthur as their own – that's how stories work.

There was a great king in Winchester, though, and we've already met him in another story, and that was the Saxon king of Wessex, Alfred, and people often confuse Alfred with Arthur.

So here is a story that begins with King Alfred and a great feast. Now King Alfred held quite a lot of great feasts, which is one of the reasons why people rather liked him, not least because he didn't just invite the posh people.

Alfred decided to have a feast for all the craftsmen in his kingdom – and he decided to give a reward to the one who would be described as 'the father of all the craftsmen'.

Well – they all rolled up; the tailor, the shoemaker, the carpenter, the blanket-maker (very important in a draughty castle with no glass in the windows), the curtain-maker (important for the same reason), the stone mason, the chef, the brewer, the butcher, the baker, the wheelwright, the scribe, the cooper, the bagpipe-maker – and the blacksmith. Everyone kept a bit of a distance from the blacksmith, because he wasn't very clean, and he was scruffy and angry-looking. Sometimes he reminded people of those old gods, or the gods of those terrible, raiding Danes – Thor with his hammer, beating sparks from his anvil in the sky.

Well, they all sat down to the feast – and Alfred, king and scholar, sat at the head of the great table. He looked truly royal, because he was dressed in a gorgeous new gown, made for him by the tailor. The gown was lined with fur, and decorated with pictures that told of the events of Alfred's reign, from the burning of the cakes to the final great victory over the Danes at the Battle of Edington.

At the end of the feast Alfred stood up, resplendent in his gown, and, using the embroidered pictures as illustrations, told stories of the battles between Saxon and Dane.

He then declared the tailor to be the father of all the craftsmen, and all the other craftsmen, with the exception of the blacksmith, felt that there could be no argument with this, because who else could make a wondrous gown that could tell the story of the Kingdom of Wessex?

The blacksmith, however, stood up and growled. He was the only one with the courage and independence, or maybe fool-hardiness, to do so.

'None of you would be anywhere without me,' he snarled, 'not one of you, including you, your majesty.'

There was a sharp intake of breath from everyone at that, speaking disrespectfully to the king; and the guards' hands went to their sword hilts.

'You would use those swords, would you?' sneered the blacksmith, 'Swords made by me.'

'You push things too far, blacksmith,' said the king. 'You dwell in a kingdom where there is peace for you to do your work and make more than swords. You have displeased me; leave us and go back to your forge.'

And so that is what the blacksmith did. All the other craftsmen lived within the city walls of Winchester, but the forge was outside the city in a hamlet by the river, a meeting place of two fords, something which gave it its name of Twyford. The smith went back there and sulked. He sat down underneath a yew tree in the churchyard and muttered, 'To hell with them – I'll starve – I'll do nothing – I'll let the forge fire go out – I'll leave the bellows alone and see if all the hot air that comes out of Winchester can work them.' So the blacksmith went into a black sulk, and glared at his own boots.

There was no problem at first, but then Alfred's horse threw a shoe, and there was no one to put on a new one. The tailor's pins started to wear down, and there was no one to make new pins. The baker's shovel wore through and he couldn't get a new one for putting loaves into the oven. The shoemaker needed a new awl, the butcher needed a new knife, the carpenter needed a new saw, the stonemason needed a new trowel, the wheelwright needed new rims for the wheels, the cooper needed new bands for his barrels – the only one who had no problems was the bagpipe-maker, but then it was generally other people who had a problem with him.

So they all went to the blacksmith's forge in Twyford, and tried to create these things for themselves. Firstly they thought they'd better shoe the king's horse, but he kicked the cooper in the hoopers, then the tailor burnt his fingers, the butcher dropped a heavy piece of metal on his toe and destroyed a brand-new pair of clogs made for him by the shoemaker, the carpenter dropped a red-hot horseshoe on his toe and started to jump around the forge, shouting and swearing – they all crashed into each other, and then blamed each other, and then started to fight. *BANG!* They knocked the anvil over.

This was when King Alfred arrived at the forge.

'*ENOUGH* – you silly, moon-faced bunch of clods,' he bellowed. 'Bring the blacksmith back – he is the father of the craftsmen.'

So they all went to the yew tree in the churchyard and brought the smith back to his forge, and to show there were no hard feelings, he made each of them a present. There was a baking tin for the baker, a hammer for the shoemaker, a chisel for the stonemason, nails for the carpenter, hoops for the cooper and the wheelwright, a knife for the butcher and some new needles for the tailor – oh, and a brand-new, shining crown for King Alfred's wife, Queen Ealswitha.

Then Alfred told them all to sing a song and the blacksmith sang a song called 'The Blacksmith's Song'. He sang it so loudly that he blew the crown off Queen Ealswitha's head, but that is the way to sing a song properly – full blast, and none of that twiddling around and whining and moaning and pretending to be all sensitive.

The tailor though, he was cross and resentful that the accolade of being father of the craftsmen had been taken from him, so he crawled under the table and snipped at the blacksmith's apron with his scissors, and this is the reason why blacksmith's aprons are all raggedy round the edges – something that really doesn't bother blacksmiths one little bit.

After this time the citizens of Twyford celebrated 'Clem Supper' every 26th of November – Saint Clement being the patron saint of blacksmiths, and 26th November being his special saint's day. Everybody would have a few drinks, sing some verses of 'The Blacksmith's Song' (very loudly), then they would get some gunpowder, stuff it in a hole in the anvil, and set light to it. This would make a really loud BANG, which would remind everyone of the time the craftsmen had a fight and knocked the anvil over.

This custom died out in the 1880s – I think because of the carnage that occasionally happened when they stuffed too much gunpowder in the hole, and blew up the anvil. I suppose it was a bit dangerous.

Fun, though.

PART TWO
WHEN THE DEVIL CAME TO TWYFORD

Well, one day the blacksmith was in his forge when the Devil came wandering by. The Devil often wandered the roads of Hampshire, and in those days you could wander down a country lane without fear of being hit by a car.

The smith had just shoed a horse, and, as always, had made a good job of it. You might think that nailing iron shoes to a horse's hoof would hurt it, but it doesn't cause any pain if it's done properly. The blacksmith of Twyford was so good at his work that the horse felt all light on its hooves, and started to dance up and down the lane, skipping and jumping, whilst the beaming blacksmith looked on with satisfaction.

The Devil looked down at his own hooves – because the Devil does have hooves as well as horns – and thought about how worn away they were with all that walking around Hampshire looking for souls that he'd been doing. Well – why shouldn't he get the blacksmith to make him a fine new set of shoes?

So the Devil pulled his hood up over his horns, and with his eyes glowing red from inside the darkness of his cowl, he entered the forge.

'I want you to put a couple of your finest shoes on me, and I want as good a job as you did on that there horse,' said the Devil, 'and get on with it, blacksmith, or it'll be the worse for you.'

'Sorry,' said the blacksmith, 'I don't shoe devils.'

'Who said I'm a devil?' screeched the evil one.

'Who else would have hooves?' observed the smith.

'Well, you can shoe me – or else I'll drag you down to hell.'

'You can try,' thought the blacksmith, but he said nothing, he just caught hold of the Devil's leg. But the Devil has cloven hooves like a goat, quite different to a horse – and as the blacksmith hammered in a nail the evil one screamed with pain.

'Ow – stop – you're hurting me!'

'Why should I stop, Devil?' bellowed the smith. 'You like to cause pain; now here's some for you.'

The Devil twisted and struggled, but he couldn't escape the smith's vice-like grip – he tried to prod the blacksmith with his toasting fork, but the smith just laughed and knocked it away with his hammer.

'*STOP!*' howled the Devil. 'I'll give you a wish … a wish.'

'I want special stuff to stick things.' The blacksmith could weld metal to metal, rivet wood to metal – but he couldn't glue wood to metal.

'I'll give you the recipe,' screamed the Devil, 'then you must let me go.'

So the Devil told the smith how to make glue out of horses' hooves, the blacksmith pulled the nail out of the Devil's hoof – and the Devil hopped all the way to Portsmouth, where he put his hoof in the water with a hiss of steam.

Well, time passed and time passed, the blacksmith grew older, and so did everyone else; and one day Death came to the forge.

'You've lived a long and useful life,' said Death, 'and now it's time for you to come with me.'

'I haven't trained an apprentice to take my place,' said the blacksmith.

'Well, you've had time enough for that,' said Death.

'I wasn't planning on dying just yet,' said the smith.

'That is not your decision,' said Death. 'Your time has come.'

'Well, Death, why don't you sit down on that chair, whilst I finish making this weathervane for the church tower, and then I'll be ready to come with you.'

So Death sat down on a wooden chair, but the blacksmith had smeared the seat with the Devil's special hoof glue – and Death was trapped.

'Ha ha, Death,' shouted the blacksmith. 'Now you can't wrap anyone in your icy arms. We can all go on living and loving, smithing and singing, drinking and dancing, and I don't need to train an apprentice.'

So – no one died. The elderly grew older, birds fell out of trees and then hopped back up again, farmers tried to slaughter animals for the butcher but the animals got back up again, houses grew fuller and fuller, and King Alfred's beard grew down to the ground and trailed along behind him. The old were weary and tired, and more and more people became old – and the people clamoured for the return of Death.

The blacksmith felt worn down by care and responsibility, and he made himself a pair of iron shoes, and walked all the way to hell via Portsmouth.

The Devil peeped round the gates of hell, and squealed, 'You stay out of here.'

'Please,' pleaded the smith, 'give me the secret to free Death.'

The Devil needed souls, and he was scared of the blacksmith, so he shouted, 'Water, you fool. Water dissolves hoof glue – now go and release Death; but when Death takes you, don't be coming down here, because I don't want you.'

So the smith plodded back to Twyford and used water to release Death. Death was ready to run around, wrapping her cold arms around all those waiting people, but she shouted at the blacksmith, 'I don't want you.'

And so the Twyford blacksmith can never die – he wanders the highways and byways of Hampshire forever. For hundreds of years there was work for him – he was often to be seen in one of those lonely smithies outside a village – but then came mass production and there was less call for blacksmiths.

Probably he's a welder now, and I have seen one such person working from an industrial unit round the back of the Danestream farm shop, near Hordle. His ravaged face and haunted eyes make him look as ancient as time itself – so maybe he is the Twyford blacksmith – doomed to immortality: the fate worse than death, because it is a fate in which there is no death.

8

LOVEY WARNE
AND THE
TRIP TO
JERUSALEM

In the eighteenth and early nineteenth centuries anyone importing luxury goods into England from abroad had to pay very high taxes: goods such as wine and brandy, tea and tobacco, fine lacework and fancy silks. So, in order to avoid these taxes, people smuggled them into the country.

In 1774 the writer Daniel Defoe wrote about the Hampshire port of Lymington, 'I do not find they have any foreign commerce, except it be what we call smuggling and roguing; which I may say, is the reigning commerce of all this part of the English coast, from the mouth of the Thames to the Land's End in Cornwall.' So smuggling was big business all down the coast of Hampshire.

In the hamlet of Knave's Ash, between Crow and Burley, there lived a woman called Lovey Warne. She'd been born there, and grew up with her brothers, Peter and John. They were all active smugglers, or 'free-traders', as they liked to call it. Smugglers would run the boats from France into Christchurch and Highcliffe, and Lovey and her brothers would carry it, using New Forest ponies, up to hiding places in the forest during the night. Sometimes Lovey would wrap the silks and lacework around her body, under her skirts and bodice, so that no revenue officer could know that she was carrying them. The revenue officers were the customs men, there to police the coast and catch smugglers, and the smugglers called them by the not very flattering name of 'shingle kickers'.

As Lovey grew older, she grew more portly, because she loved her food and her brandy and ale – but, on occasion, she looked even more portly, because of all the fancy goods she had wrapped around her person. Sometimes, indeed, she would carry great skins full of brandy or wine around her middle, and she'd make a sloshing sound as she walked along.

Another of her jobs was being the lookout woman. If Peter, John and the others were running contraband (smuggled goods) up from the coast, she'd stand on Verely Hill, which is near Picket Post, on the western edge of the forest. If she saw that the shingle

kickers were about, she'd put on a bright red cloak, and the free-traders would be warned.

Well, as Lovey grew older, her brothers passed away – and Lovey herself became queen of the free-traders, though no one took the risk of calling her that.

There came a time when the shingle kickers were particularly active around Christchurch, Highcliffe and the far west of the forest, so the free-traders started to run the goods in further east down the coast, at a secret spot called Pitt's Deep, over towards Lymington.Pitt's Deep is a beautiful place, and if you go there nowadays, even in the height of summer when the New Forest is full of visitors, you'll never find many people there. There's a long shingle beach and a glorious view over to the Isle of Wight. There are a few houses there, and one used to be the Forge Hammer Inn, and it was a notorious smugglers' haunt. No doubt this was because the landlady was Lovey Warne herself.

Well, there'd been a grand shipment in from France, and the smugglers had roped the brandy kegs together, and sunk them just offshore at a place called Brandy Hole. They would come back to get them when the coast was clear – for they knew that the shingle kickers had ventured down to Lymington from Christchurch, and they were led by Chief Riding Officer Abraham Pike, a man widely feared by the free-traders.

Just one keg had been brought ashore and tapped – so they could drink some, and bottle some for the people who had helped them, or who had looked the other way when they passed. The vicar was due to visit, and Lovey had some brandy for him.

It was just like in the poem 'The Smugglers Song' that Rudyard Kipling wrote:

> *Five-and-twenty ponies,*
> *trotting through the dark–*
> *With brandy for the Parson*
> *and 'baccy for the Clerk.*
> *Laces for a lady, letters for a spy,*
> *And watch the wall, my darling,*
> *while the Gentlemen go by!*

(Sometimes people called smugglers 'the Gentlemen' –
it helped to keep things secret.)

So, you see, the vicar was as involved as anyone else, and he liked his fine French brandy.

Well, most of the free-traders had disappeared off into the forest, so Lovey sat down at the table for a fine feast of ale, brandy, bacon and Jerusalem artichokes. Oh, she loved those Jerusalem artichokes. Jerusalem artichokes are a vegetable a bit like a knobbly potato – they don't come from Jerusalem, and they aren't really artichokes, which is a quite different vegetable. They grow easily, and Lovey Warne had a whole patch of them growing round the back of the Forge Hammer Inn. The only problem is – well – it has to be said – they do make you a bit windy.

In 1621, the Hampshire botanist John Goodyer had written that 'which way soever they be dressed and eaten, they stir and cause a filthy loathsome stinking wind within the body, thereby causing the belly to be pained and tormented, and are a meat more fit for swine than men'. I suppose this meant that he didn't like them, but Lovey Warne thought they were quite fit to eat. It is said that if you add the seeds of the herb 'lovage', that can take away the flatulent effects – but Lovey swore by the cleansing effects of the Jerusalem artichoke, so Lovey wouldn't add lovage, though she did like lovage leaves in her brandy.

After Lovey had polished off her meal, the door opened, and in, rather nervously, came the vicar. Lovey locked the door after him.

'The Lord allows me some brandy to assist my reflections, and some tobacco to smoke whilst I talk to the Almighty,' said the vicar rather guiltily.

'I have both for you, your reverence,' said Lovey with a wink and a wicked smile. The vicar placed the brandy bottles and the tobacco into a bag, which he hoisted on to his back – just as the door handle rattled, and someone tried to open the door. Finding it locked, they hammered on it thunderously.

'*OPEN UP, IN THE NAME OF THE KING,*' bellowed the well-known voice of Abraham Pike. 'We have you surrounded.'

'It'll take plenty of your men to surround me, Abraham Pike,' roared back Lovey Warne.

'Oh my Lord,' squealed the vicar, 'I cannot be found here, oh what would the bishop say? Oh, where will I hide these things?'

Lovey knew that the shingle kickers would search the inn from top to bottom, so she said to the vicar, 'Only one place for you to hide, my luvver; under my skirts.'

The vicar looked both shocked and horrified. 'Oh, 'tis decent, your reverence, I have many layers to protect my modesty'… and indeed she did – Lovey wore bloomers the like of which, if hoisted on a mast, would sail a ship to America and back again, and they were covered in pockets designed to hide all forms of contraband goods.

There came a huge crash at the door that nearly burst it open, and the vicar, knowing there was no other hiding place, ducked underneath Lovey's skirts.

'Hold there, my pretty boys,' shouted Lovey. 'Are you that desperate for a drink you'd drag a woman from her dinner?'

She shuffled towards the door, walking being difficult with the vicar crouching under her skirts. She unlocked the door, and in came Abraham Pike and his band of shingle kickers.

'Well, Lovey Warne,' said Pike, 'I have reason to believe that you have smuggled goods on the premises.'

'Me, Abe?' said she. 'Surely you know that I'm a God-fearing woman that would never do anything contrary to the law.'

'Oh, 'tis so, Lovey,' said Abraham Pike, with a knowing grin in spite of the serious nature of his duties.

'Go on then, boys,' he ordered his men, 'take the place apart, I want every cupboard, every hidey hole, gone through.'

'You're a terrible fuss,' said Lovey. 'Now, would you want a bite to eat?'

'What is it you have?'

'Lovely Jerusalem artichokes – they say that eating them brings you closer to God; every bite is a step closer to Jerusalem.'

'Fartichokes!' roared Abraham Pike. 'You'll not have me eating them, Lovey Warne, the wife would throw me out of house and home.'

'Please yourself,' said she. 'I swear by them; nothing better for clearing out the system.'

'Why don't you sit down?' said Pike. 'The men will be a while searching out your contraband, and then you'll be a'walking to the goal house.'

'I'll be a'walking nowhere,' said Lovey, 'and I generally have to stand after a meal of Jerusalem artichokes.'

PARP...

... came a noise from beneath Lovey's skirts, and this was followed by something that sounded like a strangulated cry.

'What was that?' exclaimed Pike.

'What?'

'I heard something, coming from beneath ...'

'ABRAHAM PIKE. Are you saying that I passed wind? A lady never passes wind, and a gentleman would certainly never point it out.'

'No, no, not that. Something afterwards.'

'Ricochet,' she said – and then *FLUMFF* - a more soggy-sounding guff, followed by a

groan of such agony and despair that had surely never been heard since Saint Michael cast the evil one out of heaven.

Abraham Pike took out his handkerchief and pretended to be blowing his nose, whilst really trying to protect himself from the aromatic waves that swept towards him.

'Good God,' he thought to himself, 'guffs that have such power, they echo with the sound of the very devils dancing in hell.'

Lovey Warne now had a slightly pained expression on her face, and as she put her two hands to her stomach, there came a rumbling from beneath that sounded like a storm at sea advancing towards a full-rigged ship, as the sailors rush to the yard arms to haul in the sails.

'*THAT'S ENOUGH!*' bellowed Abraham Pike. 'Search over, boys, there's nothing here – we're away back to Christchurch, and we'll take the coast path, through the good sea air.'

After the shingle kickers had gone, the unfortunate vicar emerged from beneath Lovey's skirts, and it is said that he was green as a frog. He staggered back to the vicarage, looking a bit like a frog crawling round a pond.

Well, the vicar didn't remain in the parish long after that – he took another parish as soon as possible, and I believe that this was the parish of Windlesham in Sussex.

As for Lovey Warne, queen of the free-traders – she lived a good, long life – a testament to the beneficial effects of ale, brandy, bacon and Jerusalem artichokes.

9

POMPEY, THE DEVIL AND THE DEEP BLUE SEA

PART ONE
CHIPS AND THE DEVIL

They do like a grim story in Portsmouth, and if the Devil comes into a Portsmouth story, no one gets the better of him like the blacksmith did in Twyford. Maybe the Devil comes from Portsmouth, and being a sailor on one of those Royal Navy sailing ships in the days of Nelson must have been like living in hell – the close quarters below decks, the stench and the lack of hygiene, the scrambling around the rigging in all weathers, the maggoty salt beef and weevil-ridden biscuits, the rationed brackish drinking water, the cat-o'-nine-tails – and then, when the ship went into battle – the noise, the shattered eardrums; the shattered bodies from shot, chain, splinters, cannonballs; the decks awash with blood. No wonder there was a press gang to kidnap men to serve aboard these hell ships – no one in their right mind would sign on voluntarily.

Working in Pompey dockyard (Portsmouth people call their city 'Pompey', I don't know why, but then, neither do they) was no picnic either, though better than going to sea in one of His Majesty's ships.

Once upon a time there was, in Pompey dockyard, a carpenter called Chips – well people always call carpenters 'Chips' – and his father, grandfather and great-grandfather before him had all been great carpenters – but they'd owed a lot of their greatness to the fact that they'd sold their souls to the Devil. The price the Devil had paid for their souls was an iron pot, a bushel of sixpenny nails, a half-ton of copper and a rat that could speak. None of them had wanted the rat, he was just a nuisance, but they'd wanted the rest. Well an iron pot was useful and expensive, a bushel was a whole lot of nails, and copper was wondrous and handy stuff. At that time the Royal Navy was 'copper bottoming' all her bigger war ships – copper protected their hulls from corrosion and being eaten by shipworms.

Now, it was one day when Chips was all alone, down in the dark hold of a seventy-four-gun ship called the *Argonaut*, that the Devil paid a visit. The Devil had round staring eyes that shone in the darkness below decks, and sparks flew out of his mouth when he spoke.

'A lemon has pips, a dockyard has ships, and I'll have Chips,' said the Devil, who was always rather fond of speaking in rhyme.

The Devil held an iron pot, and next to him was a bushel of nails, and on the other side of him was a half-ton of copper. Sitting on his shoulder was a rat.

'What you want, Devil?' said Chips.

The Devil didn't answer, so Chips ignored him and carried on working.

'What you doing, Chips?' asked the rat.

'I'm putting in planks, where you lot have eaten them away,' answered Chips.

'Oh, we'll just eat them too,' said the rat, 'and then the ship will sail away, sink, and all the crew will drown.'

'Oh will you indeed?' said Chips. 'Well, that's as maybe, but a job is a job, and I've got a job to do.'

But Chips couldn't keep his eyes off the iron pot, the sixpenny nails and the half-ton of copper.

'You know the deal,' croaked the Devil, 'same as for your father, your grandfather and your great-grandfather.'

'Yes, but I don't want that rat.'

'You want the rest – you get me,' squeaked the rat.

So Chips thought to himself, 'I'll kill the rat and have the rest,' so he agreed to the deal, and the Devil disappeared in a puff of smoke.

Well, Chips sold the nails and the copper, and he thought to himself, 'Now I've got enough money, I can marry the corn chandler's daughter.'

But he couldn't sell the pot, because whenever he offered it for sale, the rat would pop out.

'Right, rat, I'll kill you,' thought Chips.

So one day, whilst working at the dockyard, Chips saw that the rat was in the pot, and he poured boiling pitch into it. Pitch is black and sticky, like tar, and is used for caulking up the gaps between ships' planks. Chips then sat and watched the pitch harden. After this he went to see the smelter, the man who produced copper, and he put the pot into the smelter's furnace. When it came out of the furnace it was white hot, and the pitch was steaming like hell itself. Out popped the rat, stuck its tongue out at Chips, and said, 'A lemon has pips, a dockyard has ships, and I'll have Chips,' after which it gave a terrible, squeaky laugh.

Well after this things turned from bad to worse; rats kept popping out of everything Chips had anything to do with. They popped out of his pocket, swam in his beer, stood on his head, peeked over his pillow when he was in bed, and jumped out of the old wooden toilet when he sat down on it. Worse, though, was when he put his arms around the corn chandler's daughter. Rats ran out of his sleeves, and hid in her bodice, burrowed into her hair, and jumped up and down on top of her hat. Naturally enough she screamed and shrieked, and completely changed her mind about marrying Chips.

Well, all this sent Chips quite mad, and he was forever walking around and shouting at

the rats, and he got careless with his work –
so one day the press gang came, and took him
for a sailor.

The ship they took him to was the *Argonaut*,
and she sailed out of Portsmouth Harbour,
over the Spithead anchorage, and out to sea,
with an enormous rat sitting on her figurehead.

One night, out at sea, Chips awoke in his hammock, and the rat was sitting on his head.

'We're nibbling through, and we'll drown the crew,' the rat whispered into Chips' ear.

Well, Chips went to the captain, and he said, 'Sir, your honour, sail for the nearest port, or the ship will go down.'

'Are you mad, my man?' said the captain. 'The nearest port is Le Havre, and I'm not going there.'

'You must, sir, your honour,' pleaded Chips, 'if you ever want to see your family again. The rats are down there now, and they're going "nibble, nibble, nibble", and when they're not nibbling they're laughing and singing that they're going to float to France on our dead bodies.'

'The poor fellow has gone completely mad,' said the captain to the quartermaster, 'take him to the doctor, and see if the doctor can knock some sense back into his noggin.'

So Chips was dragged off to the doctor, and whilst the doctor was examining Chips, and tapping him on the noggin with a small hammer, the rats nibbled right through the bottom of the ship, in poured the sea, the *Argonaut* sank, and everybody was drowned.

One particular rat floated ashore on top of Chips' body, or what was left of Chips' body. When the startled French people pulled the body ashore, the rat upped and said, 'A lemon has pips, a dockyard has ships, and I've had Chips,' but the people didn't understand, because the rat couldn't speak French.

Well, that's not a very nice story, but then it does come from Portsmouth. I first read it in a book of folk stories, but when I investigated further, I found that it had been written down in a book called *The Uncommercial Traveller* by Charles Dickens. Dickens, however, claimed it was a folk story – in his book he writes that it was told to him when he was little, by a woman who was looking after him. In his story he says her name was 'Mercy', probably because she wasn't really having much mercy on the little boy she was terrifying.

The histories suggest that she was called Mary Weller. Dickens was born in Portsmouth, where his father worked as a clerk in the Royal Navy pay office, but when Charles was little the family moved to Chatham in Kent, taking Mary with them. Chatham was a dockyard much like Portsmouth, though this story is set back in old Pompey.

So, it is a folk story because Dickens says it is – though I do wonder a little bit whether he made it up – I gather that there are some writers who make stuff up, and that this drives the people who collect folk stories completely round the bend.

If he did make it up, however, it is because it is along the lines of all those grim Portsmouth stories, stories that Pompey women would use to frighten the living daylights out of small children.

Read it, though, as written by Charles Dickens. I'd read the story as I found it in a folk tale book first, but I loved his version. I suppose you have to get used to a certain old-fashioned way of writing, but that's part of the pleasure. I'd much rather read it as written by Dickens, than as written by me!

PART TWO
JACK THE PAINTER

As far as I know, which isn't very far, Dickens never wrote about Jack the Painter. Jack the Painter was a revolutionary, and his real name was James Hill, though it might have been James Aiken, or then again, James Hinde. He was a Scotsman who came to work in Pompey dockyard, and, as you may have guessed, he worked as a painter. There was plenty of painting to be done on those old wooden ships, both inside and out – and just look at those glorious yellow and black stripes on HMS *Victory*.

This was in 1776, during the time of the American fight for independence from Britain, and Jack sympathised with the rebel American colonists. So – he decided to strike a blow against the Royal Navy.

Now, if you look at a picture or model of an old-fashioned square-rigged sailing ship, you'll see that the ship couldn't be worked without miles and miles of rope: the rigging. In Portsmouth dockyard there were very long buildings called 'rope houses', which are now museums, where the ropes could be stretched out as they were made. So Jack, looking to cause maximum damage, set fire to the rope houses. The fire was put out, though, and Jack was captured.

Well, I don't suppose he had much of a trial before they hanged him. They took the mizzenmast of a ship called the *Arethusa* (the mizzen is the mast closest to the stern), erected it outside the dockyard gates, and that's where they hanged Jack. It was all very public – the authorities wanted the people to see what would happen to revolutionaries. There was revolution in America, revolution threatening in France, and the powers that be were afraid of revolution in England.

Jack's body was tarred and gibbeted – that means it was covered in tar and put in an iron cage – and the cage was hung up from a gallows on Fort Blockhouse, a place that guarded the entrance to Portsmouth Harbour. This meant that as the ships sailed in and out of Portsmouth, the sailors would all see the body. The authorities were afraid of mutinous and revolutionary behaviour from sailors, and indeed there was a great mutiny at Spithead, the anchorage just outside Portsmouth Harbour, in 1797; so this fear wasn't an unfounded one.

However, sailors aren't so easily cowed, and one night some drunk members of His Majesty's Royal Navy (well, this is Pompey) nicked a rowing boat, rowed out to Fort Blockhouse, and stole the skeleton of Jack the Painter. They then sold bits and pieces of the skeleton to the landlords and landladies of pubs throughout Portsmouth; well, Pompey people are a gruesome lot and love that sort of thing: 'Oh, I've got a rib from Jack the Painter, that'll bring the customers in!'

The prize part of the skeleton was the skull, and they flogged that to the landlady of the London Tavern, which was just opposite the very place where Jack was hanged. It was knocked down a long time ago now, though there is another pub there, called the Ship Anson.

Well the trouble was, not only did the pub get the skull, it also got the ghost. Folk didn't always worry too much about that, sailors are never too fussy about who they drink with, but the room upstairs was a lodging, a hotel for rather grander people, including merchants and the wives of ships' officers – and Jack, being a revolutionary and, by his own reckoning, a champion of the common people, liked to clank and clatter about, and give them a really good fright. In consequence, the London Tavern was losing custom.

Fed up with this, the landlady took the skull down to the docks, and lobbed it into the briny.

Jack didn't seem to be too upset by this – his ghost just started to cause mischief all the way around Old Portsmouth – usually to those who might consider themselves a bit high and mighty. He still does it.

Sometimes he clatters around the road by the old sea wall, and if there's someone important staying in one of the guesthouses, he peers through the windows and grinds his teeth. That scares the living daylights, or should I say nightlights, out of them, something that always seems to give him satisfaction.

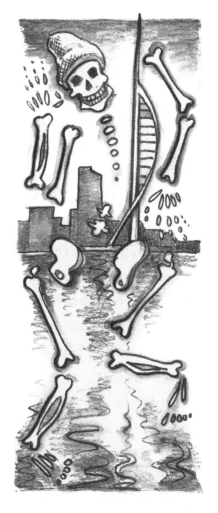

In the 1980s marine archaeologists were busy salvaging the wreck of the *Mary Rose*, a sunken Tudor ship that had sat at the bottom of the harbour since long before Jack the Painter was born. A very important person was invited down to Portsmouth to have a look, and so he joined the diving team over the wreck. The lead diver told everyone to stick together; the waters there are murky and gloomy, and it is important that divers behave in a safe manner. However, the very important person wasn't used to being told what to do, so, on a whim, he left the team and swam off in a different direction. This was the perfect opportunity for old Jack. Slowly he rose from the seabed, and gnashed his teeth at the very important person, whilst howling in a most terrifying manner. They say that ever since then the very important person has been quite mad – but no one can tell him so, because he is, after all, a very important person.

Another of Jack's more recent pranks was the most noticeable of all. By the side of Portsmouth Docks there is a wondrous construction called the Spinnaker Tower, built in 2005. It used to be a pure sunlight white, which suited its graceful, soaring form, but one night, in 2015, Jack crept out of the sea, and – he is after all, a painter – painted its legs blue. The once graceful tower now looks like it's wearing blue socks, something that amuses Jack the Painter, who likes to see the mighty look fallen.

So – mischief around Pompey Docks – and it's all likely to stem from the ghastly, skeletal ghost of Jack the Painter:

Whose corpse, by ponderous irons wrung,
High upon Blockhouse Beach was hung,
And long to every tempest swung?
Why truly, Jack the Painter's!

Whose bones, some years since taken down,
Were brought in curious bag to town,
And left in pledge for half-a-crown?
Why truly. Jack the Painter's!

That's a poem written in 1820, by a poet called Henry Slight. Everyone's forgotten poor Henry Slight, except, that is, for these verses, and you won't hear them anywhere much except Pompey. That's because, to this day, old Jack's bones still go a'clattering around the old dockyard.

10

THE STONES OF ROTTEN HILL

There seems to be a tradition of walking stones in Hampshire. In the village of Farringdon, near Alton, there are some stones which are said to be a young couple who went for a walk, and a kiss and a cuddle, on a Sunday. Kissing on a Sunday! What a sin. For this they were turned to stone, stones still seen alongside Brightstone Lane in the village. Sometimes, on a Sunday, the stones have a little stroll.

Then there are the three stones that gave their name to Three Stone Copse in Titchfield. It was said that every so often they'd cross the road and settle for a while on the other side. You would never actually see them move, but you would never know what side of the road they would be on in the morning. One night they wandered to an open wooded space at the side of West Street, and they've been there ever since. You can go and have a look.

Then there were the three stones that used to sit at the foot of Bevois Mount in Southampton, the place where Sir Bevois himself was reputed to be buried. Every so often they used to wander into a pub called the Bevois Castle Hotel, and have three pints whilst no one was looking, but then some new owners changed the name of the pub, and the stones, shocked at this disrespectful insult to tradition, disappeared and were never seen again.

Then, by the side of the Silchester Road, on the border between Hampshire and Berkshire, there is the Imp Stone. Some people say that every midsummer night, at midnight, it turns into an imp, and hops all the way to the treacle mines at Tadley, where it causes chaos by pouring the treacle everywhere, and singing songs out of tune. Other people say that there was an imp that used to shout very rude things at a giant called Onion, who lived in the old Roman city of Calleva Atrebatum, and one day the giant threw a rock at the imp and flattened it – so the stone is actually on top of the imp, and if you look you can see the giant's fingerprints on its sides. I don't know which story is true, so you'd better go there yourself and have a look – then you can make your own mind up.

And then – as if we needed any more – there was once a stone circle at a place called Rotten Hill, near the village of Overton. Probably there were once stone circles all over Hampshire, but over the years farmers ploughed up the land, and people took the stones to build houses, barns and churches.

In neighbouring Wiltshire a lot of the stone circles survived, possibly because the local people were too lazy, drunk and feckless to put them to the good use that hard-working Hampshire people did. Avebury and Stonehenge are famous, whilst others, like Marden, have lost their stones but still have the embankments, and were once as spectacular as Avebury. The area in the middle of Wiltshire – Salisbury Plain, the Vale of Pewsey, and surrounding regions – must have once been the centre of a great culture, and many roads must have led there.

Many of these roads crossed Hampshire, and one was The Old Way. This ancient track lead from the seaports of Kent, and the city of Canterbury, all the way across the land to the port of Seaton, in Dorset. In medieval times the eastern part of the The Old Way became a pilgrimage route, called The Harrow Way, along which pilgrims walked and rode from Winchester to Canterbury.

The Old Way goes past Rotten Hill, near the village of Overton. Once upon a time (so the stories say) there was a stone circle on Rotten Hill. I want to tell you a story about this stone circle, but firstly I need to tell you about the Overton Sheep Fair. Overton was an important central place for Hampshire and the surrounding counties, and shepherds would bring their flocks there for sale. Drovers, men who take sheep or cattle over long distances, would bring flocks of sheep to Overton along The Old Way. The drovers were tough men; they had to cope with driving these flocks for hundreds of miles, protecting and caring for the flocks as they did so, sleeping out in the open in all weathers, and dealing with robbers and thieves. On occasion there were drovers who were not incapable of a bit of robbing and thieving themselves.

One such drover arrived in Overton, after droving a flock of sheep for a farmer in faraway eastern Sussex. The drover had originally come from Whitchurch, a nest of thieves and rogues not so far from Overton, but the innocent Sussex farmer trusted him, and never dreamed that the drover might never return – taking all the money that the sheep would fetch at market.

The sheep were auctioned, and the drover, with a purse full of money, fell into the appalling and licentious pubs of Overton, some of the worst dens of iniquity in Hampshire.

After several days' drinking, and eating masses of pork scratchings, all the money was gone, and he staggered out of Overton and fell asleep upon a hill. The hill was Rotten Hill, and he was in the middle of the stone circle.

Now, the day was the 7th of July, and it was the day of the Feast of Thomas of Canterbury. In medieval times this was an important saints day, and thus important for The Old Way – which did, after all, lead to the holy city of Canterbury. The Overton Sheep

Fair was always held round and about that date – perhaps it had always been a special date, even before the arrival of Christianity, some sort of a mid-summer festival. It was said that on that day the stones could talk.

It was a grating, grinding sound that woke the drunken drover.

'How be you, Long Maggie?' said a stone.

'Oh, I spose I could be worse,' replied Long Maggie.

'I'm looking forward to a bit of a stroll,' said another stone.

'Not long to go, only another six months till Twelfth Night,' said Long Maggie.

The drover, rigid with terror, pretended he was still asleep.

'What be that stinking heap of rags and putrefaction that be lying in the middle of our circle?' said a stone.

'Some drunk human. I expect he comes from Whitchurch.'

'Well, 'tis a good thing it's not Twelfth Night, he might watch us walk down to the river for a drink, and steal our treasure.'

The drover was befuddled with drink and fear, but his ears pricked up at the mention of the word 'treasure'.

> *'Gold and silver*
> *and precious stones,*
> *Emeralds and rubies,*
> *and drover's bones'*

sang a stone.

> *'Iron and loadstone,*
> *and blood from the sky,*
> *And death to the thief*
> *who comes wandering by'*

sang another.

> *'The treasure of Arthur*
> *and Alfred and all,*
> *And the skull of a thief*
> *turned into a ball'*

sang two more stones together.

'A game of football
up on the hill,
With standing stones playing
and treasure there still'

sang another four.

'And I'll score a goal
and head it right in,
Amidst gold and silver,
and Cornish tin.'

sang the centre forward.

Well, the drover wasn't listening to all the words – all he could hear was 'treasure', and 'silver', and 'gold', and 'emeralds', and 'rubies', and 'Cornish tin' – Cornish tin was once brought along The Old Way to the sea ports of Kent, bound for the Continent; it was the most useful of all.

Finally, after midday had passed, the stones stopped talking, and the drover crept away.

The next day he was back, with pick, shovel and grub axe. All day he dug and heaved under a stone: Long Maggie. Back he came, day after day, till he finally toppled the stone. In the pit where the stone had stood, he found a gold ring. It was a wondrous ring, but he had expected more.

'Nothing else for it,' he thought. 'Sell the ring, and wait for Twelfth Night.' Well, we know about Twelfth Night from the first chapter, it's a special night when trees and stones walk, animals talk, and mulled cider is drunk by the gallon.

So – on the evening of Twelfth Night, the drover hid himself in a copse, up on the hill, next to the stone circle.

As the church clock in Overton struck the midnight hour, the stones started to judder and move, and then, rolling and crunching, they circled the fallen form of Long Maggie. Angry scraping sounds came from them, though they said no words, as they helped her upright; after which they started bumping down the hill towards the River Test.

The moon was full, the eyes of the drover were as round and wide as the full moon, and they were even wider when he saw the treasure glinting in the moonlight, for the top of the hill seemed to have opened. As the stones disappeared over the brow of the hill the drover darted forwards and started filling his sacks with treasure.

As he scrabbled at the treasure he saw a golden bell – a beautiful object, covered with elaborate patterns and engravings. He grabbed it, but put one hand inside to hold the clapper and stop it ringing. But grasp it as hard as he could, he couldn't stop it from moving – firstly it vibrated a little bit, then more, then it started to swing from side to side, the drover's hand was jerked from the clapper, and the bell rang out – loud and shrill upon the hill.

There was a growling and rumbling, and the drover looked up to see the stones surrounding the hole in the hill.

'*THIEF!*' groaned one.

'*ROBBER!*' creaked another.

'*BURGLAR, STONE-TOPPLER!*' growled Long Maggie.

… and they started to jump up and down, until the whole hill was vibrating.

The drover gave a scream of terror as the top of the hill fell in upon him – and then drover and treasure – disappeared into the earth.

'Well,' said Long Maggie, 'I don't want to stay here now, Rotten Hill is ruined for me.'

… and so off they set – the stones bumped, thumped and ground their way along The Old Way – all the way to Stonehenge. The stones of Stonehenge, however, were a bit snooty and full of themselves, what with their lintels and capstones and famousness and wotnot, so the stones of Rotten Hill left The Old Way and lurched up to Avebury, because they knew that there was a village called West Overton there, so the stones reckoned that they had come from East Overton. Avebury didn't seem quite the place for them, though, a bit overcrowded, so they followed Woden's Dyke, a great long earthwork now called the Wansdyke, into Somerset.

Eventually they arrived at the place where stood their long-lost cousins, stones they hadn't seen for ten thousand years – this was a place called Stanton Drew – and there they stayed.

At Stanton Drew, below the hill,
If they're not gone,
They stand there still.

As for the Overton Sheep Fair – with the decline of sheep farming, and mechanisation, and the development of road transport, it eventually died out.

However, in the year 2000 it was reinvented by some imaginative, committed and stalwart Overton people. I know this because I told stories there – it is a fair that now takes place every four years, and I've been to every one. So – depending on when you are reading this, the next one will be in 2020, or 2024, or whenever! You can probably count better than I can. I'm always there, telling tales, so look out for me and ask me for a story, and, by the way, if you go for a game of football on top of Rotten Hill – keep your eye on the ball.

I would be much obliged if you would also tell your parents to buy me a pint. Thank you very much.

And here we come to the end of the book: from Twelfth Night to Twelfth Night.

If you take any of these stories and tell them to someone else, I would be delighted. I don't mean read them aloud, though that is also fun, but tell them from memory. Don't try and learn them, like an actor learning lines, but tell them your own way and in your own words. You'll forget all sorts of bits, but then you just put in your own ideas, and the story changes, and becomes yours. Then, you can start discovering other stories; there are loads more folk tales in Hampshire, and millions in the rest of the world.

Then, you too will be a storyteller. I'm getting a bit old now, and keep going to sleep when I'm in the middle of telling a story, and sometimes people throw things at me to wake me up. We need to see some new, young storytellers, storytellers who can stay awake and not start snoring in the middle of a tale.

BIBLIOGRAPHY

BOOKS

Beddington, Winifred G., and Christy, Elsa B., *It Happened in Hampshire* (Hampshire Federation of Women's Institutes, Winchester, 1937, revised 1948)

Dickens, Charles, *The Uncommercial Traveller* (First published 1861)

Ekwall, Eilert, *The Concise Oxford Dictionary of English Place Names* (Oxford University Press, 4th revised edition, 1960)

Foss, Michael (ed.), *Folk Tales of the British Isles* (Book Club Associates, London, 1977)

O'Leary, Michael, *Hampshire and Isle of Wight Folk Tales* (The History Press, Stroud, 2011)

Thoms, William John, *Gammer Gurton's Famous History of Sir Bevis of Hampton* (Wiley and Putnam, New York, 1846)

Thoms, William John, *Gammer Gurton's Famous History of Sir Guy of Warwick* (Wiley and Putnam, New York, 1846)

WEBSITES

Andover Museum
hampshireculturaltrust.org.uk/andover-museum

Jack the Painter
porttowns.port.ac.uk/dead-men-telling-tales

Lovey Warne
www.thenewforestguide.co.uk/history/
new-forest-smugglers/

Michael O'Leary
www.michaelolearystoryteller.com

www.facebook.com/Michael-OLeary-Hagstone-
Storyteller-196027053927350/?fref=ts

Overton Sheep Fair
overtonsheepfair.co.uk

Su Eaton
su-eaton.co.uk

Society *for*
Storytelling

Since 1993, The Society for Storytelling has championed the ancient art of oral storytelling and its long and honourable history – not just as entertainment, but also in education, health, and inspiring and changing lives. Storytellers, enthusiasts and academics support and are supported by this registered charity to ensure the art is nurtured and developed throughout the UK.

Many activities of the Society are available to all, such as locating storytellers on the Society website, taking part in our annual National Storytelling Week at the start of every February, purchasing our quarterly magazine Storylines, or attending our Annual Gathering – a chance to revel in engaging performances, inspiring workshops, and the company of like-minded people.

You can also become a member of the Society to support the work we do. In return, you receive free access to Storylines, discounted tickets to the Annual Gathering and other storytelling events, the opportunity to join our mentorship scheme for new storytellers, and more. Among our great deals for members is a 30% discount off titles from The History Press.

For more information, including how to join, please visit

www.sfs.org.uk